PERFECT
BOOK

A DOUBLE SHOT OF MAGIC

JO-ANN CARSON

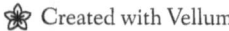

"I have measured out my life in coffee spoons."

~ T.S. Elliot

A Double Shot of Magic

~ *a recipe for love* ~.
The Perfect Brew Trilogy, book 2
By Jo-Ann Carson

When evil rises, one witch must save the world. Darkness seeps into the small Pacific Northwest town of Mystic Keep, a haven for supernaturals and unsuspecting humans, the kind of place where everyone has a secret. Cassie Black, the owner of The Perfect Brew, a café that serves coffee laced with magic, and protector of the inter-dimensional portal beneath it, fights the darkness with the help of her unusual posse of men, and kid sister, Jane.

Larry, a popular homeless man with a mysterious past, is shot in an alley. Clenched tightly in his hand is a note, "BEWARE BLACK WITCH." The words, written in blood, could mean many things, and none of them are good. As Cassie unravels the mystery of his death, someone tries to murder her.

The very human detective, Gavin McGregor, suspects Cassie is the cause of all the unusual happenings in town and shadows her every move. Her former boyfriend, Alessandro, the vampire, wants her back in his life, alive or dead, and makes his intentions clear. Sanjay Kahn, a wickedly handsome, rogue warlock, vies for her attention and her heart.

A murder to solve, a supernatural curse to wrestle with, and a full dance card ... what more could a good witch want?

A Double Shot of Dead is the second book in the critically acclaimed Perfect Brew trilogy. It can be read as a stand-alone or as part of the series. If you like magical cozies with strong characters, romance, and humor, you'll love this novel.

Buy *A Double Shot of Dead* today and enjoy a fun, heart-warming story filled with intrigue and sweet romance.

ONE

"All things are possible with coffee and mascara." ∼ Koffee
Addict, Facebook

On the first sunny morning of June, Cassie Black woke up
with a splitting headache and a craving for strawberries
dipped in dark chocolate. Rubbing her forehead, she sat up
and spoke to her familiar. "I just got a warning dipped in
chocolate. Something is wrong."

Sid rolled her eyes and toggled her head from side to
side. "You need to relax, Cassie. Witch up. You've been
ridiculously busy ever since we came to this town. You need
..."

Cassie stopped her cat with a stink eye. Familiars could
be worse than mothers when it came to scolding.

A silver fog flooded the room, capturing their attention.
In the middle of the mist, the renegade warlock Sanjay
Kahn appeared. Thoughts of chocolate vanished from
Cassie's mind.

Sid purred.

Cassie grumbled.

Even without his dramatic entrance, Sanjay had a formidable presence. His perfectly sculpted face was a delicious composite of sharp angles and mysterious shadows. As if that wasn't tempting enough, mother nature had graced him with the lean, muscled body of an athlete. He had an intoxicating scent, which made lovers swoon. Worst of all, he had the charming ways of a tomcat.

Sanjay swaggered towards her bed, and her heartbeat raced north of normal, even for a witch. His wavy, mahogany-brown hair fell to an impressive set of broad shoulders clad in brown leather. His skin, the color of café au lait, glistened with energy, while his marmalade eyes blazed with power. He stared down at her.

Cassie gritted her teeth. Despite her many misgivings about Sanjay, and warlocks in general, his presence raised her pulse. She knew he could sense this. Witch biology was annoyingly transparent. But, not a hint of his usual cocky grin appeared. Instead, his lips pressed together in a long, firm line that signaled trouble. She sat up straighter.

As he towered over her bed, she gripped her bedsheet to anchor herself.

"We've got a problem," he said.

"Don't you ever knock?" she said.

Scanning her body slowly, he heated the room ten degrees. "I need your help," he said.

Had Sanjay the great, or at least he thought he was great, asked for help? Wanting to savor the moment, she stretched her legs and wiggled her toes. Yup, she was awake.

The charmed, silver mist had dissipated in the room, but the warlock's expansive magic remained. It smelled like warm cinnamon toast on a cold winter morning.

Sid continued to purr.

The traitor thought Cassie. She took a deep breath and said to Sanjay. "Wait in the living room. I'll be right out."

He squinted. "You know I've seen you naked. Right?"

"Thanks for the reminder."

His smile flickered. "Cassie, I'll never forget."

She hit him in the head with a pillow. While his voice sounded cool, she sensed an alluring animal heat behind his words, one that awakened parts of her, she did not want awake.

Her cheeks burned. "Just wait for me, hotshot." She tossed another pillow at him for good measure. He deflected it with magic.

WITH A FLICK OF HER WRIST, Cassie used magic to dress. Looking in the mirror, she felt somewhat pleased with the result. Over a pair of tailored black pants, she wore a moss-colored, cashmere sweater that accentuated her green eyes. Her blond hair fell in a neat, classic bob that framed her face. Her lipstick was a soft pink shade rather than a passionate red.

Her look would have been perfect if her sweater had not ended up backwards. Manually, she fixed her blunder. She shook her head at her reflection. It was no wonder her family called her the clumsy witch.

Her migraine was gone, but in its wake, a dark sense of foreboding had settled on her shoulders. Since when did any warlock admit he needed help? Especially this warlock —the powerful Sanjay Kahn? What could she possibly do for him that he could not do for himself? He was so proficient in magic, and she was so not.

. . .

CASSIE JOINED Sanjay in the living room of her well-appointed apartment, which sat above The Perfect Brew coffee shop, which was a haven for the supernatural. She had inherited both from her great-aunt Ophelia along with some other interesting things. She sat on a blue, velvet wing chair opposite him.

Sid lay at Sanjay's feet. Double traitor, she thought. The feline raised her head to acknowledge Cassie's entrance and purred.

"Okay, so what's up?" Cassie asked Sanjay once she settled in.

"We need a schedule," he said.

Cassie felt her eyes widen. All this fuss over a to-do list? "Seriously?" she said. "I hate lists."

He sighed. "I understand you like to live on the wild side, but considering our responsibilities, we need to make a plan."

Good grief! He wanted to talk about guarding the portal at this time in the morning. She grumbled.

His eyes bored into hers as if they were lasers in need of target practice.

"A plan?" she said. She didn't like parroting people, but she needed time to think. Being a guardian of one of thirteen portals on earth was a position of grand-gravitas in the supernatural world, but it was not something she had ever wanted. Just thinking about it made her squirm. Why had her eccentric great-aunt passed such a great responsibility on to Cassie's shoulders? Any one of her five sisters would have been a better choice. It made no sense.

The fact that she had to work with Sanjay made even less. At times Cassie swore she could hear the universe cackling at her. She stretched her neck.

"Yes." Sanjay continued, "Now that our basic protection

spells are firmly in place, we need to make a plan to sustain them." He cleared his throat. "On even days, I'll strengthen the wards. You get the odds."

Great, I get to be the odd one, she thought. "I need coffee," she said out loud.

Ignoring her comment, he continued talking. "On the first day of every month, we'll use our combined magic to do an assessment of our security system and plug the leaks."

Combined magic? "I really need coffee," she said.

"I've made a chart," he said. "All you have to do is put a checkmark in a box, each time you strengthen the portal gates. If you see any problems, you write a note in the orange comment section. If it's a big problem, you contact me immediately."

A chart. "I really, really need coffee," Cassie said.

Sid slinked over to Cassie, leaped onto her right shoulder and curled her tail around her neck. Cassie soaked in her cat's compassion, but it wasn't enough.

Sanjay snapped his fingers, and a file folder appeared in his hand.

A file folder. Shoot me now, she thought.

"Here's a paper copy of this month's schedule. We will enter the information on an app on our cell phones, which logs the data into a database, which we can then print out. I named the app, 'Portal Keep.'" He leaned towards her, offering her the file as if it were a treasure.

Cassie didn't take it. "You created an app." She squeezed her eyes so tightly she saw stars.

Sanjay leaned back. His face fell. "I hoped you would like my solution. I know you find my company uncomfortable at times. This way, we don't have to meet so often."

Where should she start? "First things first, Sanjay. I'm still just getting used to living here in Mystic Keep." She got up and walked to the front door of her apartment. "I'm going downstairs for coffee."

THE PERFECT BREW looked like every other independent coffee house on the corner of every other downtown street, in every other small town in America. Warm and friendly, it buzzed with caffeinated patrons. Soft jazz played over the speakers, and a hum of chatter filled the room. Italian espresso machines steamed at the bar. The line-up never ended, as it was the most popular coffee house in town.

The Brew offered everyone's favorite shots and a variety of great coffee beans. The only thing different about it was that magic enhanced every drink and the air smelled of enchantment.

Cassie took her usual seat at a table by the fireplace, where a wood fire burned. The warmth of the flames and the crackling sounds of the burning logs calmed her nerves. She had hoped Sanjay wouldn't follow her, but her luck had never been that good. He appeared instantaneously, using magic rather than the staircase, and sat down opposite her. His file folder made a plopping sound as it fell on top of the table between them. He folded his arms. "Is it that time?" he asked.

As in, that time of the month! How dare he? She shook her head. It was, but that was beside the point. "Sanjay, you don't get it," she said.

He leaned forward and grasped her hand. A familiar jolt ran through her body. It happened every time he touched her. Cassie's mind said it was a result of his magic touching hers, a witchy-power thing, but her body begged to differ.

"Tell me," he said.

His tiger eyes turned a hot orange, and she found herself talking. "I like Mystic Keep. I do. It's a pretty little Pacific Northwest town with interesting people. It..." She sighed. "It just wasn't part of *my* plan. I've never liked small towns, and now I am stuck in one. It's suffocating me."

Sanjay made a face. "You're wrong. It suits you," he said. "And you know it. You just don't want to admit it yet, but this town is your true home." The cinnamon scent of his magic enveloped her, caressing her vulnerability. "So, cut the untruths. Tell me what's bothering you."

"Well, maybe it's not the size that matters."

He snickered. Cassie knew he would.

"The size of the town, that is," she said. "It's my role here. When I lived in Amsterdam, one of the more beautiful culturally diverse, and interesting cosmopolitan cities in the world, I was an artist. I had a growing reputation for creating Van Gogh replicas, and I made good money. It may not have been legal, but that's beside the point. I got paid for creating good art. Now I'm a caffeine pusher in a town no one has ever heard of. Did you know Mystic Keep is not even on some maps?"

Sid jumped into her lap.

Sanjay squeezed her hand. "Need I tell you that you are far more than the owner of a café? You protect one of thirteen portals that connect our world to other dimensions. And your shop is a haven for supernaturals. Without it, they would roam this land with no sanctuary." His right brow rose. "And Mystic Keep rocks, in its own magical way."

She shrugged.

Oscar, the Brew's head barista, delivered her coffee, an enhanced cup of heaven made of finely brewed beans from Brazil, laced with a delightful mixture of magical herbs. He had designed it to give her energy and perspective to start her day. She took her hand from Sanjay's and smiled at the kitchen witch. It wasn't hard. Standing over six feet tall, he was blond and built like a warrior. Behind his back, the women in the town called him Thor. A kitchen witch by birth, he was a master of potions, and his brew always hit the spot. Good to the last magic drop, she thought. She cleared her throat. "Thanks, Oscar. You're the best."

"I bet you tell all the men that," Oscar said. He winked and turned to Sanjay, who was his best friend. "You treat her well, warlock." Before Sanjay had a chance to say anything, Oscar vanished and reappeared behind the coffee bar.

As she took her first sip, she felt Sanjay watching her for a reaction. Did she sigh? Maybe. She couldn't help it. The brew tasted that good. Like the first glass of water after walking in the desert, like the first piece of meat after a vegan diet, like the first time with a lover. That good.

After her second sip, Sanjay leaned towards her. "Okay. I get it. You're not in the mood for business this morning. Just promise me, you'll look at the paperwork," he said.

"The Portal Keep App." She nodded. "Got it." She gave him a glimmer of a smile, but he didn't look convinced. "I promise I'll take a look." A calm settled over her. If Sanjay wanted check marks on paper, it wouldn't be the end of the world. To make their business-slash-friendship work, she would make compromises. Right? And this one little app wasn't a big deal. Just two strokes of a pen. She took another sip of her heavenly elixir.

The bells on the front door rang, heralding the entrance of a mundane. Everyone inside turned to look. Some glamoured themselves to look more human. The volume of conversations lowered, and the smell of incantations from a witch table disappeared. Sunshine, and salty air laced with the sweet scent of cherry blossoms poured into the room

Larry limped in. He favored his right leg, the one with the bad knee, which needed replacing. Being homeless, he spent his days on the street. Judging by the deep wrinkles worn into his face, Cassie guessed him to be in his forties. He wore dirty, blue jeans, and a Raptors tee-shirt soiled with grease. His salt and pepper hair stood in clumps as if it had been cut with a chain saw. His dark brown eyes stared out at the world with hopelessness. A week of scruff covered his cheeks. If he were twenty years younger, he might have looked cool in a rock 'n roll, emaciated sort of way. Being older, he simply looked forlorn, as if he had lost his step while the rest of the world kept spinning. He walked up to the bar and ordered a coffee from Brianna, his favorite barista.

The first time Cassie saw Larry enter The Brew, she had questioned Brianna's practice of giving him a free coffee. After all, Cassie was running a business. Brianna told Cassie not to worry. The shop made enough money to keep running, and its purpose wasn't monetary. When Cassie checked her sales stats, she found Briana was right. The coffee house was doing well financially.

Rain or shine, Larry limped through the front door every morning. Holding his drink as if it were gold, he turned away from the bar and scanned the room for a free table. Cassie waved him over. They were becoming good friends.

Sanjay waved his hand above the file folder, making it disappear. Cassie sipped her coffee and felt better and better. Sanjay telepathically asked Oscar for a brew.

Larry sat down with them. "Good Morning," he said.

His scratchy voice would have worried Cassie, but she

knew his drink would heal it within minutes. "Good Morning, Larry. How's it going, on this beautiful day in paradise?"

He took a sip. "Funny, you should ask." He smiled at her. "I could use your help."

They stared at him. Larry usually regaled them with stories about his bird watching or a controversial news item in the New York Times, which he read daily at the Barber Shop. In the three months she had known him, he had never asked her for anything.

"I'm starting a campaign," he said.

They leaned in.

"A 'Clean the Keep' campaign," he said with authority as if he were running to be the next mayor. "We need this." His voice was hushed. "There are rumors, you know, about odd things happening in town. I don't believe any of it. Not me. Uh uh," He shook his head and gulped his coffee. A drop of fluid slid down his mouth and trickled through his whiskers. He swiped at it with his grubby right hand. "We're losing our sense of community, and that's making people distrust each other. If we all work together, we'll be happier. Cleaning the streets is a good place to start."

Wowsers thought Cassie. People knew strange things happened in town! The supernatural community did it's best to keep a low profile. She knew there had been rumors, but she had hoped they would die off.

For Larry to be worried, it had to be getting bad out there. The mages needed to make stronger cloaking spells. She looked at the warlock.

Sanjay straightened his back. "Count me in," he said. "Let me know where and when and I'll be there. And I'd be happy to bring a couple of boxes of plastic gloves."

A warlock picking up trash? Cassie stifled a chuckle.

"Me too," she said. "The Brew will contribute garbage bags."

"I knew I could count on you guys. You know some idiots think this place is the source of trouble. I tell them that's just not true. Any place that can brew coffee this good can't be bad." He chugged the rest of his drink and smiled as magic flowed around him.

Sanjay's left brow rose. "I can't argue with that, my friend."

TWO

Sanjay returned to his home, which he shared with George, an ornery ghost, and his familiar, a peregrine falcon. The manor, perched on the edge of a cliff, looked as if it might fall into the ocean. He had chosen the run-down five-acre estate because it was situated at the end of a road few knew about.

As soon as the door closed behind him, he spoke to his AI device. "Edward, order two hundred plastic gloves to be delivered to Mystic Keep asap," Edward repeated the order.

The house smelled of magic and dust. No matter how many times Sanjay used spells to sweep out the cobwebs, they clung to the old place. Sunlight streamed through the cracks in the Venetian blinds, adding to the cold feel of the rooms. At one time, the manor held an elegant, twenties, Art Nouveau vibe, evident in the stained glass windows. Now it felt austere and haunted. It's forbidding aura suited the life of a rogue warlock who cherished his solitude.

In 1920, George Carroway, a wealthy man who had made his money on the railroads, purchased the property and built a large estate house with ocean views. He wanted to impress his new wife, who was twenty years younger than himself. When she ran off with the gardener, whose prowess in the boudoir was legendary, he tried to hang himself from the rafters in the attic. But they broke. Two years later, his mistress poisoned him, hoping to inherit his fortune. Unfortunately for her, she left way too many clues and ended up hanging for her deed. The remains of the country manor crumbled over the years with disuse. No one wanted to live so far out of town, in a house with such a horrid beginning, and a troublesome ghost.

Yes, George Carroway became a ghost.

Three decades later, Clive Carroway inherited the property and spent a tiny fortune renovating it into a small Inn called Carroway's Hideaway. It had one or two good reviews in the newspapers at the time. Still, he struggled to make a go of it, due to the high cost of maintaining a drafty manor with poor plumbing and wiring. It didn't help that George Carroway's ghost enjoyed playing tricks on visitors. After Clive went bankrupt, the house sat empty for decades.

Sanjay purchased it the day after his first visit to The Perfect Brew a year ago. He believed in Ophelia's dream of creating a sanctuary for supernatural beings in Mystic Keep. After spending years traveling, he needed a place to call home. The Carroway estate drew him. The sandstone building had three solid stories, more room than he could ever need. It had an overrun garden that he could put to use, and two turrets that rose into the sky. The amazing views of the cove sealed the deal for Sanjay. Magic and a bit of money could fix it up nicely.

George, the ghost, was another matter. Their relationship was an on-going battle of wits. The first month Sanjay endured the sound of chains scraping on the floor through the long hours of the night, and he woke up every morning to find his clothing moved to other parts of the house. Sanjay ignored George's shenanigans figuring he would get tired of his tricks sooner or later.

But George did not. One day he hid Sanjay's grimoire, so Sanjay retaliated by placing spells on sections of the house so that George could not enter them.

George, infuriated at being kept out of parts of his own house, began to moan twenty-four-seven.

Sanjay ignored him and carried on with his life. For now, they were at an impasse.

The manor had seven-bedroom suites: one on the main floor, and three larger suites on the others. A large industrial kitchen, dining room, and study were on the first floor. With magic, Sanjay sealed the basement where he maintained his laboratory. The attic he left to George. Someday, he would fix the whole place up, but that day had not arrived. A year had passed.

Sanjay clicked his fingers to warm his home. Wanting time and solitude to think, he went to his favorite chair by a large window in his west turret.

The morning had not gone as planned. Why did Cassie have to be so stubborn? Witches!

If the two of them set up a routine, the weight of their responsibility for protecting the portal would lighten. Why couldn't Cassie see that? Maybe he should have asked her after her morning coffee.

· · ·

THE IMAGE of her body slid across his mind, and his memory traced her rounded curves. Delicious curves. He shook his head. His heart sank. He couldn't go there. He used magic to get himself a beer.

His familiar, a peregrine falcon flew into the room. "You have bigger things to worry about than your love life warlock," he said.

Sanjay nodded. "Peregrine, I don't need a lecture from you."

"Darkness is coming." The falcon had a sinister voice.

It always does. His bird wasn't saying anything new. "Nothing sinister has happened for three months," Sanjay said to the bird. "Three months."

"Three months," repeated the falcon. "What does that say to you?"

Sanjay growled, not wanting to admit to the truth. "Okay. Okay. Darkness never disappears on its own. I know. It lies low and waits for an opportunity to strike again."

"And so ...?" Peregrine said.

"We're in danger."

THREE

"*I'm not afraid of monsters. I'm afreaid of the coffee maker breaking.*" ~ Koffee Addict, FB

Three days later ...

Cassie lay back in her bubble bath. Sid lounged above her on the windowsill soaking in the late afternoon rays.

"I never want to hear the word "trash" again," Cassie said.

Sid opened one eye. "How about 'checklist'?"

Cassie threw a washcloth at her.

With the agility, only a cat familiar could muster, Sid evaded the wet mass and chuckled. "Didn't you say something to the staff about us all needing to do our part? About hiding the fact that we're different? About setting an example?"

Cassie sunk under the bubbles. She had made more than one of those speeches, which led to her spending hours physically picking up garbage. Never had she imagined a town as small as Mystic Keep could gather so much crap. Cassie had speared moldy orange peels on the main street, scooped-up dirty diapers in vacant lots, and grabbed greasy, fast-food wrappers from the steps of city hall. And then there were the alleys. She shivered, not wanting to step into one ever again. Usually, mages used magic to clean up messes. This time she wanted all the supernatural folk to dig in and work alongside the normals.

Never had she imagined it could be so hard to act mundane.

As her head emerged above the water line, Sid said, "You made your bed, witchy. Now you need to clean it." She cackled.

"Very funny." Cassie got up and using magic dressed on her way out the door. She appeared outside The Perfect Brew, two minutes later, wearing an old pair of jeans, a sweatshirt, and red bandana. Her head gear's logo read "Keep it Clean," in white lettering. It didn't matter what Cassie wore. At the end of her cleaning shift, she would be filthy dirty.

Larry stood, waiting for her. "Good morning, sunshine," he said.

If she didn't know better, she would have thought the man had grown three inches. His eyes sparkled. He liked watching birds, reading a chatting to people, but nothing made him look this happy

"Where are we working today?" Cassie asked as she fell into step beside him. Larry carried the master plan in his hand. Good goddess, how she hated men with plans.

"A major alleyway."

Oh, goddess have mercy. "Didn't we work that yesterday."

"No, that was another alley. This one is in a neglected part of town on the outskirts." The line of his chin firmed.

"And you know, the leaders of this campaign should be seen doing the hard stuff every day."

Cassie did a double-take of the man limping beside her. He wore the overalls she had washed, and a new shirt Sanjay had given him. His hair and skin looked clean, and he had shaved. Who knew garbage could be so powerful?

Cassie smelled the alley before they entered it. Urine, pigeon poop, and vomit, the unholy triad. Just lovely. She cringed at the sight of a used needle leaning against a brick wall where a small child could easily reach it. Using a set of long tongs, she picked it up and bagged it separately as medical waste.

"Larry, do you use drugs?" she asked.

"I use weed sometimes, but I've never been interested in hard drugs. I rarely drink either. I don't like chemicals messing with my brain. It's hard enough to keep it working right." As he talked, he bagged a pile of greasy, fast-food wrappers and a pop can.

So much waste!

In the morning sunlight, Cassie narrowed her eyes. Sometimes life didn't add up. "I don't understand Larry. How did a nice guy like you end up on the streets?" She had asked him this question before, but he always evaded answering. Now that they knew each other better, she hoped he would open up.

His eyes shifted away from hers, looking for more garbage. "It happens," he said with a double nod.

The polite thing to do would be to stop asking, but Cassie's curiosity got the better of her. "Did you get sick or something?"

He grunted as he snagged a used condom from the ground. "More like something."

Now she had to know. "I guess you get asked about being homeless, a lot."

"Yup." The rubber made it to the garbage bag. "You ask a lot of questions, Cassie."

"Sorry. Talking helps pass the time." A rat ran along the edge of the building, and she screamed.

Larry laughed.

Rats shouldn't bother her, but they did. Any rodent or creepy-crawly thing scared the hex out of her, especially when they popped out of nowhere. She wiggled her nose. "How about this. I'll tell you a story about me, and you tell me a story about you."

Straightening his back, he gave her a sidelong glance. "As long as I get to pick the stories."

She nodded and began. "I grew up in a big family. I have five sisters, three parents, and numerous aunts and uncles. All on the weird side."

"That's a lot of estrogen under one roof," he said. "Were your parents trying for a boy or something?"

"It would seem so, but they never complained. We're a happy family for the most part, though being in the middle, I found the teasing nasty at times."

"I get that. There were three kids in my family," he said. "All boys. I was the oldest."

"Did they look up to you?"

"Until they could beat me up, they did. That's the way boys are." He chuckled. "We had a fort in a forest near our home, and we played war for hours on end." A whimsical look lit his brown eyes, and he smiled.

"Where are your brothers now?"

He turned back to his job of looking for crap and didn't answer. Cassie figured she had gone too far. Maybe the next day, she could find out more. His story intrigued her. Larry didn't fit the profile she had of a homeless man. But who was she to think that they would all be similar? "Sorry," she murmured and speared a rotting apple.

"No worries," he said. "Here's the thing. You're looking for a nice story about how my life went wrong, about how bad luck put me in the gutter, but I don't have anything nice to tell you. I know you mean well. But shit just happens." He stopped and scratched his chin.

She waited. When Larry didn't say anything, she tried to raise the ante. "My second story. Before coming to Mystic Keep and burying myself in coffee beans, I was an artist in Amsterdam." All true. "I painted in oils." True. "Sort of like Van Gogh." And she sold her work as Van Goghs, but she didn't tell him that.

"Cool," he said. It sounds like a nice life, but I think you fit here better. You look at home." He stopped for a minute to look into her eyes. "Nothing's stopping you from painting here."

Her breath caught. Larry was right, of course, but her life had become so complicated. Before she could say anything, he continued.

"You can't let people or stuff get in your way. If you're an artist, you should be doing art."

A part of her heart crumbled. "You know, you're right." She looked away and pretended to study the other side of the lane to hide the blush she felt spreading along her cheeks. "Your turn. Tell me another story."

"Okay." He limped along as he spoke. "I grew up in the burbs, went to university, and got a job in a bank. I married Sarah at twenty-five, a good woman with a big heart. By the time I turned thirty, we had two small children and a house with a white picket fence in the burbs."

Cassie hung on his words waiting for the downfall.

"I got framed for embezzlement. Brown & Brown, the company I worked for, didn't have enough evidence to convict me, so they fired me instead. One of the top managers must have been siphoning the money, and they made me their fall guy. Anyway, my reputation was ruined. No one would hire me. I went door to door for months looking for a job, any job, but no one wanted anything to do with me. To survive, I burned through our savings, and we lost our home." He exhaled noisily.

"I'm so sorry," Cassie said. "And Sarah?"

"I grew angry, you know. Deep, deep, angry. I threw junk around because it made me feel better. One day a book clipped my wife's head. By dawn, the next day, she and the kids had moved out. I've never been able to find them."

Cassie's mind spun with questions. Who set him up? Why didn't someone take pity on him and hire him? Why didn't the wife give him a second chance? Did she have a job? But overwhelmed by the sadness of his story, all Cassie said, "I'm so sorry."

"Well, there's nothing you or anyone else can do about it now." He walked over to a brown paper bag that looked like a discarded lunch and grabbed it.

A companionable silence fell between them.

Cassie saw a pile of wet flyers. She was so excited about seeing a relatively clean pile of garbage she didn't notice the banana peel lying on her path. Her right foot slipped on the yellow mush, and both of her feet flew into the air. She landed on her butt with a hard thud. Then came the elbows and lastly her head. *Clunk.*

"Fudge," she yelled.

Falling always embarrassed her, but being on the clumsy side, she had grown used to getting up and pretending nothing happened. Except it did happen, and there were witnesses. As she put her feet under her body and began to get up, she took in the scene. At least ten people in their "Keep it Clean" bandanas looked at her with concern.

Sanjay reached her first, materializing out of nowhere. He offered her a hand up. Refusing his help, she scrambled to her feet and wiped the dirt from her jeans. Her hip hurt in a place she didn't know existed. Her neck felt stiff and sore. Worst of all, her mouth filled with blood. She must have bit her tongue as she hit the ground.

Sanjay looked worried. "Banana peels get the best of us," he said and hesitated. "Is that blood dribbling from your mouth?"

"No," she lied, and swiped at her lips, smearing blood all over her hand. Why did Sanjay have to witness her every humiliation? Lifting her chin, she turned to the others. "I'll work in the next alley." They all laughed.

If she had to be the butt of the joke, she figured she might as well make it a good one. She gave them a radiant smile with blood-stained teeth.

Sanjay waved his hands and froze the scene. "Cassie, let me help you."

FOUR

"It's amazing how the world begins to change through the eyes of a cup of coffee." ~ Donna A. Favors

Sanjay lifted Cassie into his arms, and created a portal to take her home. Dizzy and disoriented, she didn't argue. He laid her down on her bed and performed the most potent healing spell he knew, one he had learned in Katmandu. She whimpered for a few minutes and then fell into a deep sleep. Sanjay sat with her for an hour and then confident that his spell was working well, he left.

Back at the manor, Sanjay relaxed in his favorite chair by the window. Outside, long shadows grew as dusk settled into the landscape. Seeing Cassie hurt bothered him more than it should have. He might hide his feelings from others, but he knew the truth. Sanjay the rogue warlock was totally bewitched.

His feelings for her put them both at risk ... put the town at risk ... put all of earth at risk. He couldn't let emotions get in the way of what had to be done. The dark force that had slid through the portal threatened them all. It had to be stopped.

Up until now, he had managed everything in his life on his own. But things in Mystic Keep were beyond his control. His gut clenched. He needed help, but damn it all, he liked being a rogue warlock.

Peregrine perched on the chair opposite him. "And how's going your own way working for you now?"

"Not so good," Sanjay admitted.

He could send a text to other mages for help, an email, or ...

"Oh, for the love of all magic," said Peregrine shifting from one foot to another. "Send a flamer to the Brotherhood."

"A flamer's so formal," argued Sanjay. So traditional. And asking for help from the Brotherhood was a huge step.

"It will get attention," said the bird. "Face it. You need their help."

"Hmm. I'm not sure what I would say to them after all these years."

"Yes, you are." Peregrine said.

The damn raptor could read his every thought, so there was no point in lying. "Yeah, well, maybe," Sanjay said. "But the wording needs to be clear. I don't want to come off as an arrogant asshole."

The falcon laughed. "Now, you're worried about that?"

"What? What's that supposed to mean?" said Sanjay giving his bird an evil eye.

"As I recall, you slammed the door when you walked out on them twenty years ago, and you said some pretty harsh things. Words like pompous, stuffy, and old-world come to mind."

"Well, yeah," admitted Sanjay.

"Yeah." The bird nodded his head.

Sanjay exhaled sharply. "You think a flamer will get me what I want?"

"Absolutely," said the familiar.

"Okay, here goes." Sanjay waved his right hand in the air, conjured a note, and froze.

"Come on, big boy. You can do this," taunted the falcon.

As Sanjay spoke, words formed on the magic notepaper: "Dear Brotherhood,

It is with great humility... *Sanjay winced.* And an open heart. *He scrunched his face.* That I write this note. I regret. *He swallowed.* I deeply regret the way I parted from the great Brotherhood, the greatest fraternity on earth, and I request to be reinstated.

Sanjay groaned. Peregrine clicked his beak as if to applaud his effort.

I have no excuse for my behavior, except to say that I was young and stupid. I have enjoyed being a rogue warlock. But I have come to learn that a sorcerer is stronger when he stands with his brothers. *Bile rose in Sanjay's throat.*

As I'm sure you know, I have always conducted myself with integrity, and always followed the moral code of our brethren, even when I worked independently.

Now, I seek community.

Sanjay hesitated. It all sounded weak, as if he was a warlock who couldn't clean up after himself. But that wasn't the whole story. He had to explain his predicament.

Let me explain. I'm fighting a dark force I fear I can't defeat on my own. Many lives are at risk. Possibly our whole world. I need guidance. *Such a hard thing to say - he swallowed again.* And backing.

How much should he tell them?

I live in a small Pacific Northwest town called Mystic Keep. Before I came here, I lived a carefree life as a rogue warlock. I reveled in being young, powerful, and independent. I loved waking up in a new place every day. No commitments. No expectations.

That all ended a year ago when I came to Mystic Keep and met Ophelia Black. A witch-like no other, she created a haven for supernaturals, the likes of which I had not seen anywhere in the world.

On the outside it's a coffee-house. A simple coffee-house, in which any supernatural can relax and receive a magical elixir tailored to their needs and desires. Ophelia employed a team of talented kitchen-witches to create perfect potions for every individual who enters her domain. It is not only a brilliant business plan, it's also a super-humanitarian act. As soon as I drank my first brew, I knew I had found a home, and I became part of the local community.

On my second day in Mystic Keep, Ophelia asked me to help her strengthen the wards around the coffee house. We worked together for weeks, and the weeks turned into months. Each day, the aura of The Perfect Brew grew stronger.

Before either of us realized it, the coffee house took on a life of its own. At first, I didn't mind. Sentient buildings thrive all over the world. We shrugged it off, as a minor side-effect of sorcery, until the building got ornery. The Perfect Brew threw a massive hissy fit. Lights flashed, espresso machines steamed, and the air smelled fouler than a sulfur pit.

Ophelia, who had the closest relationship with the structure, spent hours calming her down and surmised that The Brew was tired of being pushed and prodded. We assured her we would be gentler with our spells and continued to craft the perfect supernatural sanctuary.

I will never forget laughing with Ophelia about how our creation had woke up as a teenager with rebellious feelings. But we didn't laugh for long. We discovered that during The Brew's hissy fit, two things happened: an inter-dimensional portal that lay below it awoke, and dark energy slipped through.

As soon as the house realized this, she cursed us to stay with her forever.

In my defense. I did not know the portal existed before this happened. I would have been more careful. *Maybe, he would.*

We searched the town for a week, but nothing had changed. I remember how anxious I felt returning to the spell work, but we were so close to being done, I didn't want to stop. A nagging feeling that something wasn't right plagued my every move, but we continued as if nothing had happened.

Ophelia died the following week. Human doctors said it was an unusual form of cancer that quickly spread through her whole body and took her life. I knew it was the darkness. I could feel it in my bones.

A week later, Cassiopeia Black, Ophelia's grand-niece, came to town. *Sanjay frowned. How much did they need to know?* I couldn't understand why Ophelia would leave everything to a clumsy witch who spent her days forging paintings. Still, I learned that Cassie was more capable than she first appeared. Within two days, dark forces tried to kill her. Sid, her familiar, saved her life by knocking a cup of poisoned coffee out of her hand before she could drink all of it.

I stole a sample of the poison and analyzed it in my lab.

It was strong enough to kill a coven of witches, but it hadn't killed Cassie. The doctors pumped her stomach, and she had a nasty hangover for a week, but it didn't kill her. That's when I knew Cassie was more powerful than she appeared.

Stormy, a sea-witch who lives in town, confirmed it. Cassie is a Puer Dei, a direct descendant of one of the council members, and I, as you know, have royal warlock lineage. The old witch told us that we have been chosen by the Elder Council to protect the portal.

So far, we've made a mess of that job. *As Cassie says, it's never a good thing to be chosen.*

This I know for sure: there is more afoot in Mystic Keep than simple magic. Our town has quadrupled in size since The Perfect Brew opened. All kinds of supernatural beings now call it home. I fear for their safety. I fear for the world's security.

Darkness is coming. It's out there. Waiting for an opportunity.

In closing, let me briefly state my request. Please, reinstate me to The Warlock Brotherhood. I promise to attend all required functions, abide by all rules, and protect my brothers.

Regards,

Sanjay Kahn

He turned both his hand's palms up to signal the note complete. It rose a foot in the air, lit itself on fire, and flew out of the room.

FIVE

"Cafforexia: a condition in which no matter how full the coffee cup is, the person doesn't believe it's full enough." (*Death Wish Coffee Co.*)

Friday, Cassie woke up dreaming of blueberries ... dipped in chocolate. An overwhelming sense of dread ran through her body, making her nerve-endings twitch. She sat up and nudged Sid, who lay snoring beside her. "Wake up. Something's wrong," she said.

Outside, a coyote howled in the distance. The morning mist blanketing the town touched Cassie's windowpane with wraith-like tendrils. A chill ran up her spine. Something was definitely wrong.

The room filled with silver fog and Sanjay Kahn materialized at the foot of her bed. "We've got trouble."

"I can feel it," she said.

His look softened as he walked over and took her right hand in his. Once again, she marveled at how many moods his golden eyes could show. But before she thoroughly enjoyed the moment, he spoke. "Larry's dead."

Her head spun as she struggled for her next breath. How could that be? Larry? He couldn't mean their friend Larry. It had to be some other Larry. "Homeless Larry, who comes into the café every morning?" she asked.

He nodded. "Shot twice in the heart."

She swallowed hard. "Who would want to kill Larry? He was a bird-loving, nice guy." Cassie's brow tightened. "Everyone likes Larry." She couldn't think of a kinder human being.

Sanjay frowned. "Evil doesn't discriminate. You should know that."

"But Larry?" He would never ever hurt anyone.

"That's not all," said Sanjay.

Oh crap. What could be worse than murder? Her heart skipped a beat. "Did the portal open?"

"No. The portal is secure. I checked it before I came to see you."

"Then what?" What could possibly make this news worse?

Sid jumped on her lap and leaped onto her shoulder, meowing her sympathies, anticipating something only a cat could.

Sanjay stared at Cassie. "The problem is in the details."

"Go on," encouraged Cassie.

"A group of boys, riding their bikes around town, found Larry in a pool of blood in the alley behind Mystic Main. You know, they were doing kid's stuff. They were shocked when they found him dead. One of them checked his pulse on his wrist, and found a crumpled piece of paper in his hand."

"A note from the dead?" she said.

The warlock nodded. "It read, 'BEWARE BLACK WITCH.'"

In the distance, the coyote howled balefully.

Her chest tightened. "That ... That's awful."

"And, it's written in blood."

"Blood?" Cassie stood and walked to the window overlooking the town. The mist had thickened, and all she could make out was a conspiracy of ravens perched on an arbutus tree. None of this made sense. Her hands trembled. "Whose blood?"

Sanjay frowned. "I don't know yet. Luckily for us, one of the boys who found Larry is a warlock named Gabriel. He's the son of my friend, Donovan O'Reilly. We go way back. I'm sure you've seen him in The Brew. Anyway ... the news got telegraphed through our community quickly."

She waited.

Your friend, the detective, got to Larry before me and locked down the area behind police tape. I can't tell you anything more about the blood unless I see the piece of paper. I considered using magic on the cop, but there were too many people around. Gabriel told me what the note said, and that it was written in blood. That's all I know. I trust Gabriel. He's a good kid."

Cassie walked back to the bed and sat on it. "Written in blood. That could mean many things." And none of them good.

"And, so could the words." Magic flickered across Sanjay's eyes, like a raging sea of orange light. He didn't need to state the obvious, but that never stopped him. "'Black witch' could mean a witch practicing dark magic, " he said. "Or it could mean a witch in your Black Magnolia coven." He paused dramatically. "Or, it could refer to you, Cassiopeia Black, the witch? You are someone to be wary of." To his credit, he didn't grin. He sat down beside her and held her hand.

"I don't like this." Cassie's cheeks burned.

"And the blood message," continued Sanjay, "could indicate a spell has gone wrong, or the sealing of a blood-pact, or a warning, or a ..."

"Vampire," she whispered. The word tumbled out of her mouth before she could stop it.

His right brow arched and he stared at her. "A vampire?"

The air between them cooled. How much should Cassie tell Sanjay? He was a silent partner in her coffee house business, and a, not at all silent, partner in guarding the portal. They had an unusual bond and an undeniable attraction. Still, most of the time, they bickered like siblings over whose turn it was to sweep Ophelia's attic where they worked on spells. Cassie owed him no explanation. She didn't have to tell him about her past.

Cassie bit her lip. On the other hand, if a vampire was after her, it would be wise to have a strong warlock at her side. And she knew, Sanjay would stand by her and defend her with his life. An oath of allegiance had never been spoken out loud, but she knew in her heart that he would be there for her.

Could Sanjay go spell-to-fang with the living-dead? Did she really want to know the answer to that question?

Sanjay broke the thick silence between them. "What aren't you telling me?"

How could she explain? She licked her lips. "We both have pasts, Sanjay. Let's leave it at that."

"And, your past involves vampires." He lifted her chin.

"You could say that." More like *one* vampire, her boyfriend of five-years, the Alessandro of Amsterdam.

Sanjay leaned closer. "I respect your privacy, but

answer me this: would vampires come after you for some reason?"

She shrugged. "That's a good question." Would Alessandro stoop to such a theatrical entrance back into her life? They were on a break. If she were candid with herself, it was possible, but not likely. No matter how mad he was, he wouldn't want to offend her, as he considered her his .... Well, there wasn't really a name for it. She thought of the possibilities: more than a lover, less than a vampire recruit, certainly not a wife, but somewhere in between all of those labels. Basically, Alessandro thought of her as his. You had to understand vampires to understand his feelings.

She shrugged a second time.

There was another risk to consider. Would any of Alessandro's enemies come after her to get to him? Hmm. They would be signing their final-death warrants if they did. Alessandro would not rest until he killed them, and theirs would be a long and horrible death. Anyone who knew Alessandro knew this. You didn't play with his toys. But vamp wars could get very messy. "I'm not sure," she said, "but I'll look into it."

"You'll look into the vampire world?" Sanjay took a deep breath, leaned back, and crossed his arms. His blazing eyes focused into the distance.

"Something like that. Trust me. I'll handle the Vamp angle."

"Trust you?" Sanjay smirked. "The Vamp angle?" He shook his head. "The more I get to know you, Cassiopeia Black, the more I know I don't know you at all."

SIX

"Coffee (N) Survival juice."

Cassie arrived at the death scene with Sid sauntering in her wake. The spring sunshine melted the morning mist. The paved alley where Larry had died ran between two main streets and was wide enough to allow delivery trucks easy access to the back doors of the stores. Large garbage bins dotted the sides. Some were closed, others, having been visited recently by binners, lay open. Food wrappers littered the ground, and the stench of rotting food hung in the air, along with a swarm of hungry flies. The warmth of the morning bounced off the pavement in shimmering waves. Three crows sat on a nearby telephone line waiting for an opportunity to feast. Cassie could feel their eyes taking in every detail. She shivered. A black rat, the size of a house-cat, skittered along the edge of the brick buildings. The walls had been tagged so many times, that no symbol stood out. The alley was the kind of place no one chose to be.

Bright-yellow police tape surrounded the murder scene, and a uniformed police officer stood by the entry point.

Cassie peered inside the cordoned-off area. Larry's body lay on the ground five yards away. Two men wearing white bunny suits covering them from head to foot, combed the area for clues. They had latex gloves, masks, goggles, and shoe booties, just like in the TV cop shows. Another bunny-clad cop took photos of the area, while another sketched the scene. It looked like the opening in a TV show. Their precision as a team felt reassuring after a murder.

A man with a stethoscope hanging from his neck knelt over Larry. Cassie recognized the tick he had in his right shoulder. It was Doc. Finnegan, the physician who worked in the town clinic next to the hospital. He had pumped her stomach a few months ago.

She looked at the other personnel at the site and shook her head. Gavin MacGregor, the drop-dead handsome guy Sanjay referred to as her friend, the cop, was nowhere in sight. She watched the investigation for a few minutes. Everyone seemed to know what they were doing and worked together like clockwork. Seeing Larry in the middle of it all was depressing.

If only she could get closer.

Sunlight peaked through the mist, illuminating the scene in bits and pieces as if it were a puzzle to be fit together. The crisp breeze off the water tasted salty. The chill in the air spoke of an incoming storm front.

Twenty bystanders gathered along the edge of the tape to watch the spectacle, murmuring in excited tones about murder. There were too many onlookers to freeze with her own pitiful magic.

She walked up to the policeman at the entry point.

"Ma'am?" the cop said. She recognized him from the café as the uniform who liked his coffee extra-hot. Oscar always smiled when he heard his order, and ladies on staff called him, 'Extra-Hot.' She had to admit he looked hand-some, with his broad shoulders, square chin and chilling blue eyes.

"Is Gavin around?" she asked him.

"He's busy."

Cops. Always busy. Cassie waved a hand in his direction and whispered, "Indica mihi absque dolo." Tell me, no lies.

Mr. 'Extra-Hot' replied, "Gavin headed back to the office to check on something. What, I don't know. He doesn't share that kind of information with me."

"Next time you come to the Perfect Brew," said Cassie, "tell the barista your coffee is on me, officer. Tell them to give you Cassie's Code 13. I appreciate all the fine work you do for our town to keep us safe. You have a good day now."

His brow wrinkled as if he were constipated, but he said nothing.

NINE MINUTES LATER, Cassie knocked on Detective Gavin MacGregor's office door in the town's, police station. He didn't answer. Using her magic, she pushed open the door and entered. The small room smelled of stale coffee. An old, wood desk with two photos, one of his dead wife and one of Marlowe, his dog, dominated the room. Two leather guest chairs sat opposite his executive leather chair. In the corner stood a wooden bookcase and a metal filing cabinet. His university degree, a picture of a group of policemen in uniforms, and a drug store calendar hung on the wall behind him.

Morning sunlight leaked between the slats of his Venetian blinds, giving the room dappled lighting, reminiscent of a noir movie set. It fit him well. Gavin MacGregor leaned back in his chair, looking every bit like Phillip Marlowe.

He's just that kind of guy, she thought: a detective with old-fashioned values. He believed in a by-the-book, right, and wrong, one-dimensional world. She sighed. While she admired his virtue and determination, she questioned his ability to see nuances. In her experience, the gray areas of life were always the most interesting. They were the places where things really fell apart.

Gavin stood up. His steely-blue eyes widened as he put his fists on his hips, making himself look more in charge, the way football coaches do, on the sidelines of a big game. He had a square jaw worth committing a crime for. His thick, curly hair had been cut short and neat. And, of course, he was clean-shaven. Although he didn't wear a uniform, his blue jeans and white tee-shirt were clean, pressed and dignified-looking. Almost six feet tall, he was a delicious-looking, lean, mean, policing machine. Cassie reigned in her hormones, as Sid chuckled in her brain.

"Hi Gavin," she said.

"Cassie, I'm ...'

"Busy. Yeah. Tell me what you know about Larry's death. She commanded the door closed and waved her hand at Gavin to loosen his tongue. "Indica mihi Deus absconsa tua." Tell me your secrets.

Gavin blinked. "I ..." His Adam's apple went up and then down, like a lost elevator car. "I ..."

"Come on, Gavin. You know you want to tell me."

His spine straightened. "Larry, a man whose last name I can't find anywhere, was shot through the heart twice, at short range, last night in a downtown alley. We don't know who did it. I'm looking for background information on him."

"And the note?"

The muscles beneath Gavin's eyes twitched as he fought against her spell. "I. Shouldn't. Tell you," he said.

"The note," she demanded.

"It said, 'BEWARE BLACK WITCH.'" All capitals. Looks like it's written in blood." He motioned with his hand for her to come closer. "That's not you is it?" he said, in a conspiratorial tone. "The 'black witch' part?" He blinked three times.

"Where's the note?" Cassie could see her tongue-loosening spell weakening. *Oh, fiddle-brooms.* Her magic had never been strong.

"I sent it to the lab," he said.

"Gavin ...."

He put his hand to his head. "Cassie? I shouldn't be telling you any of this."

She could attempt the spell again, but second spells were never as strong as firsts. Sort of like coffee. "It's okay, Gavin. You can trust me."

Gavin collapsed into his office chair and put his hands on the worn armrests. "Do you know Larry's last name?" He swiped at the sweat accumulating on his brow.

Cassie sat opposite him on one of his extra chairs and crossed her legs. "I wish."

He squinted. "Why are you here?"

A good question. "I thought it was time we had a second date," she said. And I can spell you all over again.

His crooked, boy scout smile appeared making dimples in his cheeks that made her female parts quiver. The man may be mundane, but he had serious Moxy.

She bit her lip. "I can still taste our last kiss." She didn't have to lie about that. It had been a whopper. "You know you want to see me again."

"Yes. But..." His speech sounded like an old, rumbling

engine not quite ready to kick over. Fighting against her spell had taken a lot out of him. "I'm swamped right now."

She gave him a seductive smile. "I haven't run into your car for over three months. We should celebrate."

He chuckled. "It would be fun," he admitted.

"And, for the record, officer, my last name is Black, but I'm not a black witch." All true.

His smile disappeared. "I didn't say I thought you were."

Good The detective's memory lapsed with the spell. "So, Gavin, what's the problem? Am I not your type? Have you met someone else?"

His eyes locked with hers, ticking up the heat in the room. "Let's see," he said. "Gorgeous, spontaneous, and fun to be with. I'd say you're just my type."

Sid purred.

Taking this law-maker for a spin would be fun. Awkward considering Cassie's unusual relationship with the warlock, but fun. "But?" she said.

"I have to be honest. I go to bed every night thinking about my dead wife. You don't deserve that. You should be with a guy who can totally commit to you."

"I'm not looking for forever, Gavin."

Sid snickered.

"Yeah, I understand that. But even for an evening, you deserve better."

She smiled. "Well, I have to say you have a wonderful way of turning a girl down." She played with a stray tendril of her hair and watched his eyes widen.

"I'll be honest," he said. "I hope that after my grief runs its damn course, you'll still be interested in me."

"You know where to find me." Cassie sauntered out of the room slowly, feeling his eyes on her butt.

. . .

YOU IDIOT, he thought.

As the door clicked closed behind her, Gavin smacked his forehead. How could he turn her down? Cassie Black was hot, so damn hot! Her eyes haunted him. They were an unusual shade of green he had never seen before, and they seemed to reach inside him and bewitch him. He longed to run his hands through her silky, blond hair. And then there were her curves—the kind to keep a man busy all night long.

What the hell was wrong with him? The hottest babe in town offered to hook up with him, no strings attached, and he turned her down. He ran a hand over his face. And, he had lied. Yeah, he did still think about his wife, but he also fantasized about Cassie. He wanted her. Bad. Maybe he should call her back right now. He had never had sex in the office, but why not? Maybe on his desk?

Marlowe, his golden retriever who lay curled up beneath his desk, yawned loudly. Gavin scratched the dog's head.

"Hey, buddy, she's just a woman. She's no threat to you."

Marlowe put a paw across his eyes.

Gavin sighed. "Marlowe, you just don't like her because she has a cat."

Marlowe lifted his paw and gave him a sideways, 'you-gotta-be-kidding-me' look.

Yeah, it was a dog and cat thing. But, still ... Gavin couldn't shake his gut feeling that there was something wrong about Cassie Black. She was hiding something. Larry's message had read 'BLACK WITCH,' and said 'BEWARE.' His pulse raced for a few seconds. He shook his head. How could Cassie with her angelic face be bad? How could she be a witch?

Marlowe crawled out from beneath his desk, lifted his head, and let out a soulful howl.

There was no denying that weird things happened around Cassie Black, thought Gavin. He commanded Marlowe to sit with a hand signal.

Okay, thought Gavin. He would be careful. Until he was one hundred percent sure Cassie Black wasn't a witch, or responsible for all the odd things going on in his town, he would keep her at arms-length. Even if it killed his libido.

And it was killing his libido.

It didn't help that Cassie's floral scent remained in the room. He imagined what it would be like to hold her in his arms.

Marlowe howled.

SEVEN

"Sometimes I like coffee more than people." ~ Koffee
Addict, FB

Cassie and Sid headed to The Perfect Brew. She ordered a
coffee from Oscar at the bar and headed to the back where
Stormy, her friend, an eighty-year old sea-witch sat beside
the fireplace. As they hadn't seen each other for a while,
they had a lot of catching up to do.

Stormy was knitting a yellow and blue striped knocker, a
breast prosthesis for a woman who recently had a mastec-
tomy. It was her hobby and one of her passions. She made a
basket full of them each week and took it to the local hospital's chemo unit. Her four needles clicked in rhythm, and she
didn't miss a stitch as Cassie joined her. Without looking up,
the older woman asked her, "What's twisted your broom?"

Cassie opened her hands. "I'm having a really lousy
day. I woke up with a warlock in my bedroom. Gavin
doesn't want a second date. And Larry's been murdered.
She sat opposite Stormy, to soak in the warmth of the fire.

Stormy peered over her bifocals. "Sanjay spent the night?"

"Good goddess, no. Why would you say that?"

Stormy shrugged.

"Nope." Cassie said. "No way. Don't even go there. Had you heard about Larry?"

Two wizards drinking coffee in the middle of the room stood up and pointed fingers at each other. Stormy and Cassie turned to stare. It was never a good thing when wizards pointed fingers. As they became more enraged, the glamor hiding their true identities slipped, and their power glowed.

"Do these guys always have to fight?" asked Cassie.

Stormy nodded. "The Yuskick Brothers have issues."

"Couldn't they wrestle on the floor, or play Dragons and Dungeons away from here. This finger-pointing is hard on the nerves." Cassie rose. This was the third day in a row they had done this. "I've had enough. I'm going to deal with them."

"Cassie, don't," said Stormy, but Cassie was half-way there. Oscar appeared at her side.

The two men looked alike. Deep-set wrinkles riddled their faces defined by large, bulbous noses. Their black eyes were streaked with blue lines that flickered with anger. They wore brown work-overalls and padded jackets lined with a blue-tartan, which made them look more like Hobbits from a construction site than wizards of some repute. Cassie straightened. The one sitting on the left had a scar on his cheek. "Excuse me, gentlefolk," she said.

Lightning bolts flew between the brothers, and purple smoke rose as their heads whipped her way. *Snap, crackle, and pop*. The smell of burned autumn leaves hung in the air. The last thing she wanted was a wizard war in the Brew.

Oscar touched her arm gently. "We should leave them to sort things out."

"No. It's my place. They have no right to come in here and disturb everyone." Had she really said that out loud in front of two wizards? It had been a rough morning, but she didn't have to commit suicide by wizard. They were such a moody lot.

Scar-face laughed. "So, you're Ophelia's niece. We meet at last."

Cassie's teeth chattered. She had never stood so close to so much occult power. Their potent energy pushed against every cell of her body. How did she let herself get into this situation? She was stupid. Clearly stupid. The campfire smell lingered in the room... "Yes," she said in answer to his question.

He stood up and bowed. "I am honored to make your acquaintance." His brother vanished.

"Um." Cassie looked around for the missing wizard. "I didn't want to end your conversation, but ..."

"Let me introduce myself. I am Leopold Yuskick, but you can call me Wally. That's what Ophelia called me, and I grew to like the name."

"It's a pleasure to meet you, Wally. My name is Cassie Black."

"Well, Mistress Black, let me say, I am pleased you continued this fine establishment. If I can ever be of any help to you, I am at your service." He lifted his right hand, and a flaming business card appeared. He blew the flames out and handed the card to her. The gesture was wonderfully dramatic, but the card was blank.

"If you ever need me. Hold the card and call my name."

"Thank you. That's a generous offer." Cassie swal-lowed. "But I am afraid I must talk to you about your behaviour."

The wizard's brows rose.

"Are you aware that when you and your brother fight, it scares the rest of us?"

A smile slid slowly across his face. "My apologies. We have family issues, and good lady, it wasn't my intent to bring them here. We had planned to have a nice, quiet coffee together and talk about everyday things, but when he commented on my new wife, I lost it.

"Igor has never liked her. And Eleandor, the love of my life, is a good woman. But he doesn't like her because she's part elf. He has no right to comment. His wife is part troll."

"Oscar," Cassie said.

"On it." He disappeared to work his magic on a second, special brew for Wally.

Cassie sat down. "I agree, your brother has no right to comment on your wife." Unless she was dangerous. "That must hurt your feelings." She touched his hand with hers. His skin felt cold and reptilian, but it warmed magically with her touch.

"It does, milady. It does. My wife's name is Eleandor, and you could not find a finer woman; brave of character and warm of heart. My family won't accept her because of her elfin blood."

"Families! I know exactly how you feel. My family won't accept my vampire boyfriend."

He laughed. "Love is love."

"Exactly. That's what I said."

Oscar appeared with a fresh coffee and a slice of a triple spelled double chocolate brownie. "Chocolate always soothes the heart," he said as he put the plate down in front of Wally.

Wally gave Oscar a wizardly nod. Cassie could feel crackling in the space between them, and her heart melted for the kindly wizard.

When Oscar left with new energy in his step, for he too must have been spelled. Wally took a sip of his brew and sighed. "Even better than usual."

"We aim to please," said Cassie.

He looked past her to the door. "My senses tell me another man is here for you, and he's not dead."

Cassie turned and saw Sanjay striding towards them. His eyes blazed orange. "I should go," she said. "It was a pleasure to meet you."

Wally took her hand and kissed it. A tingling warmth spread through her body. "It will be all right, child," he said. "Everything will be all right."

The words hit her hard, coming from a strange wizard, but she smiled. "Till next time, Wally."

Cassie intercepted Sanjay and took his arm to calm him down. They walked back to Stormy's table together. Cassie could feel Sanjay's fear in the pit of her stomach as if it were her own. "Easy does it, hot shot," Cassie said.

"Calm down? You want me to calm down? Do you know who you were dealing with?"

"Wally, a friend of Ophelia's."

Sanjay's brow rose. "He's one of the most powerful wizards in the realm, and not always well-behaved. The Yuskicks are a volatile clan. You should have nothing to do with them."

"Did you come to lecture me to death or protect me?" The words rushed out of her mouth. That seemed to happen when she was near him.

"Don't flatter yourself. It's not personal. I can't let anything happen to the guardian of the portal."

Okay, then. "Understood," she said, feeling ice steal into her heart.

Stormy greeted them both with a snicker. "Cassie, I wouldn't make a habit of breaking up wizard arguments. It's not good for your health," she said.

Cassie frowned. "Did you know Wally was a friend of Ophelia's?"

"Everyone liked Ophelia. You should know that by now."

Cassie leaned back. "So where were we. Stormy, did you hear about Larry?"

The older witch pursed her lips. "When I awoke I felt something was wrong, then I heard the sad news. I am sorry. I liked the man. Do you have any idea who did it?"

Oscar appeared with a large cup of steaming coffee that smelled heavenly. Before Cassie could thank him, he disappeared. She waved at him as he reappeared behind the bar.

"No." Cassie swallowed. "I don't know who did it. But it could be tied to me."

Stormy put down her knitting. "You? You hardly know the man."

"You haven't heard all the news?" So much for the gossip. "When they found Larry, he held a note in his fist, written in blood."

"Oh!" said Stormy. "That's never good."

"It gets worse," said Cassie.

"Worse?"

"It read: "BLACK WITCH BEWARE.'"

The older witch sat back and adjusted her glasses. "That could mean many things."

"Don't I know it." Cassie took a long sip of her drink.

The warmth of the fluid flowed down her throat, easing her tension, and stimulating her energy. "I think I may ask Oscar to marry me," she said.

Sanjay rolled his eyes. "You'll need to get in line behind every other woman in town." He paused. "Listen, I've been asking around about Larry. He told me he was a stockbroker who got into drugs, lost his home and his family. But his story doesn't check out."

Cassie took another sip of her heavenly brew. Oscar had written the phrase, 'Double Doozer,' on the side of her mug. She smiled.

Sanjay's eyes sparkled with power as if he sensed her response to her coffee. "I've sent out inquiries," he said. "I should know more soon."

"How did you find out he wasn't a stockbroker?"

"When I asked people around town, I found people had different stories about his past. Mostly they fell into three categories. To people like us, he talked stocks, but he told older people he was an injured war vet, and he told children he was a circus clown."

Cassie didn't bother telling him about the bank story Larry had told her. "Why would he lie?" she said out loud.

Stormy picked up her knitting. "I like the clown story, but he could be all three."

Sanjay scowled. "Unlikely."

Cassie put her half-empty cup down on the table and watched it fill itself up. "Gavin wants to know his last name."

"Gavin?" Sanjay exhaled loudly.

"He doesn't know anything about the murder, and is suspicious of everything, including me." Did her voice sound pouty? Maybe.

Sanjay's bad-boy grin came out. "He didn't melt to your charms?"

"My spell lasted three minutes," she replied, ignoring his innuendo. "It was all business."

"Uh-huh. I don't see what you see in that guy."

Stormy picked up her knitting.

"Did Gabriel sense any supernatural energy, when he found Larry?" Cassie asked.

"He says not, but he's only twelve and untrained," said Sanjay.

"I don't like this. It feels so personal. Who else can I grill? I so want to grill someone."

Sanjay stared into her eyes. "You said you would handle the Vamp-angle."

"After dark, my friend. After dark."

He tilted his head but said nothing.

Stormy pursed her lips. "Vamps? Not vamps. Please, don't let it be vamps. I hate blood-suckers."

Cassie had to change the subject before they bugged her about her connection with the undead. She had had more than enough of that kind of interrogation from her family. Not to mention the endless jokes. She must have heard every undead joke in the universe. Her sister Chloe liked popsicle jests the best. Cassie chugged the rest of her coffee and plunked the mug down. "I'm going to check out Larry's street friends." Without waiting for any remarks, undead or otherwise, she got up and strode out of the café.

Sanjay chuckled. "You know, I'll find out about you and your Vamp angle," he said to her back. "You can't keep secrets from me."

EIGHT

"With enough coffee, anything is possible."

Sid slinked behind Cassie and fell into step as she hoofed it down the sidewalk. The smell of rain was so strong she could taste it. The mountains loomed in the distance shrouded with low, dark clouds. Maybe she should start carrying an umbrella.

Sid grumbled out loud. "What's the plan?"

"My plan is to find the murderer and put an end to all the speculation." And keep Sanjay from nosing around her past.

"Cassie, that's not a plan. That's more like a declaration of war. I say you go back and make a real plan with Sanjay. And then maybe the two of you could engage in some afternoon delight." The way she said *delight* left nothing to the imagination.

Cassie grumbled.

"You know the horizontal mambo. Click your witch brooms and dance to the heat. However, you want to say it. You need some action. It's been months. Imagine what it could be like." Sid purred so loudly the air around them, vibrated with her energy.

Images flickered through Cassie's mind. She could well imagine the two of them together, and she didn't need her demon-cat to help her. "No, Sid. It's not time to play with the wicked warlock, and for that matter, it's never a good time to play with a wicked warlock. I want to find out who killed Larry."

"And clear your name."

"That too."

"And not have to tell Sanjay about Alessandro?"

"Sid, you talk too much."

The cat chuckled. "Have some respect," Cassie muttered. Did Ophelia have a spell in her grimoire to make familiars behave? When this mess was over, she would have to take a look.

Sid harrumphed and strode with her tail high.

As they meandered along Mystic Main Street, Cassie looked for clues. "This is what I know about Larry," she said in her head to Sid. "After his morning coffee at The Perfect Brew, he spent a few hours sitting on a park bench with yesterday's copy of the New York Times, which the mayor always gave him on her way to work. Sometimes he would watch the birds and talk to them. He always said hello to people who said hello to him, and sometimes they gave him food. In the afternoon, he migrated across the street to the bench in front of the barbershop. There he read paperback Westerns. Louis L'Amour was his favorite. I remember him saying, 'That man really knew how to tell a story.'"

"I'd rather talk about sex with the warlock," said Sid.

"Shush up. At dinner time, Larry went to the church, where they served hot soup. I don't know where he went afterward, but he always returned to The Perfect Brew for coffee the next morning."

"Sex. Hot, sweaty sex. With lots of moaning." Sid said as she sent her a full frontal view of Sanjay naked.

Cassie ignored him. "I wonder where Larry slept. Where he cleaned himself up? Did he have a second set of clothes? Friends? Enemies? Did he hang out at the community center?"

"You know warlocks are considered to be the best lovers." Lady Obsidian Black wiggled her whiskers with the authority of a whore house mama. "Even better than ..."

"Would you stop." Cassie groaned. "You know the more I think about Larry, the more I realize there's a lot I didn't know about him."

There had to be clues out on the street. Cassie should have asked Brianna about him. She might know more. Not wanting to return to the café defeated, she walked up and down the Mystic Main three times.

"You know you're clueless," grumbled Sid. "Even more than usual. What the hex are you looking for?"

Cassie didn't answer, because she had found it. A blond lady dressed in a well-worn, long skirt and sweater pushed a grocery buggy down the sidewalk. Piled high with clothing, a sleeping bag, and a large, dirty teddy bear, the cart wobbled. The woman wandered from side to side on the walkway.

Cassie, with Sid slinking behind her, rushed up to the woman. "Hello, my name is Cassie."

The woman's thin, weathered face leaned away. "You human?"

Cassie looked down at herself. Nothing seemed out of place. "Last time I checked." With a side of witch, of course.

"You don't look human."

Okay. "What do I look like?"

The woman leaned towards her and sniffed. "Strange. Strange, I'd say."

Cassie used all her magic to decipher if this woman had any supernaturalness about her, but she came up with nothing. "I'm sorry you think I'm strange," Cassie said.

The woman narrowed her eyes. "Watch out for the Martians. They're everywhere."

Okay then. Cassie looked around as if she truly believed aliens hid in the trees and then focused back on the woman. "You figure they won't get us if we keep moving?" she whispered.

The woman's eyes widened. "You got it."

Cassie took another dramatic look around. "If we go stand over there in the park by the big oak tree, we'll be safe."

"Really?" The homeless woman stopped.

"Yes, definitely. And I can tell you some other stuff about the aliens." Cassie bit her lip. "What's your name?"

"Ava." The woman nodded slowly. "You know, you're the first person today to believe me."

"They just don't see what we see," said Cassie.

The older woman nodded.

"How about I buy us lunch, and we can exchange information."

"Lunch?" The woman's whole body smiled for a second and then stiffened. "Why? Why do you want to give me lunch? How do I know you're not a spy? One of them?"

"I'm not and alien or an alien spy."

"You can't fool me. I've seen things in this town. Strange things."

Cassie tilted her head sympathetically. There were many strange things that happened here. The town was filled with witches, warlocks, shifters and a whole lot more.

"Last night, I saw this guy appear out of nowhere," said the woman. "When I stared at him, he winked, snapped his fingers, and handed me an apple."

Sounded like a warlock. Would Sanjay be that reckless? "Did the apple taste good?" Cassie asked her.

"It was a tart Granny Smith. Not my favorite."

"Okay, let me get this straight. Because a guy gave you an apple you didn't like, you decided there was something sinister about him?"

The woman narrowed her eyes. "Don't twist my words. I told you, he appeared out of nowhere. Normal people don't do that."

"Appearances can be ..." Cassie stopped herself from talking more about appearances in the town, and looked to the heavens for inspiration. "Did you know Larry?"

"Everyone knows Larry." Her face hardened. "I can't believe someone would kill him like that."

"Me either. I feel so bad. Where did Larry sleep at night?"

"You don't look like a cop."

"I'm not. I own The Perfect Brew, and Larry was one of our regulars. I just have to know more about him."

She nodded slowly. "I get that. We all want to know more."

"You can stop by my coffee house for free coffee anytime. Just tell the baristas, I sent you, and give them the password, Cassie's Code 13."

"Let's see what can I tell you about Larry."

Cassie pulled a chocolate granola bar out of her purse that she had tucked away for her flight back to Amsterdam. She handed it to Ava.

The woman nodded. "Larry slept in the janitor's room at the church. He had an arrangement with the priest. After evening service, Larry cleaned the main hall and the bathrooms. In exchange for his work, he got to store his stuff, and sleep on a cot in a back room."

"That sounds like a good deal."

"Larry liked it. He said the place reminded him of his childhood. He didn't look religious, but you never know what people are like on the inside."

"Which church?"

"The Catholic one, St. Frances, up on the hill." The woman tore open the bar and took a big bite. "Good stuff. Not even stale."

"Did Larry have any special friends?"

"You ask a lot of questions, lady." As she chewed, the older woman's eyes closed half-way.

"I just wish I got to know him better. That's all," said Cassie.

"If you ask me, I think the aliens did it. You see, they normally take away the quiet ones, the ones that don't fight back, but I think Larry fought back, so they killed him. He must have seen their faces."

Aliens? "Can you describe one of your Martians?"

The woman finished her bar and leaned closer to Cassie. She smelled bad. "They come at night. Dark shadowy figures. They lurk in shadows and strike quickly."

"They take people?"

"The most vulnerable."

"Uh-huh. Have you ever seen one up close?"

She shook her head. "I don't want to, lady."

"Do any of the people come back?"

"Nope." The woman looked around as if someone might be listening to their conversation.

"Have you told the police?"

"Nope."

"Why not? Maybe, they could protect you."

"All the police want is for the homeless to move on, but, lady, I got nowhere to move on to. The less they know about me, the better."

Cassie took a deep breath. What kind of a fudged-up world did they live in, that people lived on the streets scared of every shadow? Part of her wanted to feed, shelter, and care for Ava. Another part of her said that would be foolish as Ava was just one of the hundreds. The problem was too large for her to fix with a granola bar. Still, she had to do something. "Look, Ava, how about sleeping at the café tonight."

"Inside?"

"Out of the cold."

Ava squinted. "No way. It's not cold, lady. I'm not going to be lured into an unknown place. I've lost too many friends that way."

"But Ava, someone murdered Larry on the street. Aren't you worried?"

The woman shrugged her narrow shoulders. "Nah, that was something different. Either it was one of those Martians, or I don't know. Maybe his past caught up to him."

"Do you know anything about his past?"

"Everyone has a past, honey. I don't pry. If someone wants to tell me their story, I listen. Otherwise, I stay out of their space. I believe in respect."

Hard not to like this woman, even if she was a bit loony, thought Cassie. But then again, maybe she wasn't loony. Perhaps she was just more observant than most. The aliens could be ....

Cassie didn't want to think about what they could be. She and Sanjay had the portal door sealed, but it had been opened three months ago, and who knows what slithered out. "Ava, you rock. Just saying."

Cassie pulled out a second granola bar, and handed it to the woman. "How long have these shadows been on the street?"

"Poco went missing three months ago, on a full moon. She was from Port Coquitlam, and she was my bestie. We had known each other for three months."

Three months! Cassie would have to talk to Sanjay.

The woman tore the wrapper off the second bar and took a big bite. "These sure are good."

"One last question," said Cassie.

"Shoot," the woman said with her mouth full.

"Where could I find Larry's friends?"

"Kit, who came from Kitilano, was panhandling up by the hardware store a half-hour ago. He knows everybody. And you might also want to talk to the priest."

Two solid leads "Well, Ava, the offer for a place to stay stands. You come by anytime you want and ask for me. And remember, the coffee code is Cassie thirteen."

The woman's beady eyes stared at her. "I'm still not sure you're human, lady I'll be stayin' outdoors tonight." She crumpled the wrapper, put it in the pocket of her pants, and ambled on down the street.

Cassie thought about everything Ava had told her, as she watched the older woman wander away.

A priest, a homeless guy from Kitilano, and Martians, she thought.

"Sounds like the start of a bad joke to me," said Sid.

"And there were shadows!"

NINE

"I'm not saying I would die without my morning coffee. I'm just saying other people might." ~ Brianna the Barista

Cassie stood in front of the big front door of the church and considered her options. Before she could decide what to do, the entranceway opened, and a priest stepped out.

A tall, cadaverous-looking man, in a black suit with a cleric's collar stood before her. Strands of black hair had been combed over a bald spot on his head. She figured he had to be at least sixty. His beady black eyes peered down at her. "Good afternoon," he said. He offered his arthritic knobby hand for a shake.

"It might rain," Cassie said.

A shadow of a smile appeared on his long face. "I'm Jacob Greepsly. I am the priest here." The smell of sandalwood soap hung around him

Greepsly? Could that really be his name? Cassie took his hand in hers. "I'm Cassie Black. Nice to meet you."

"Ah." He gave her hand a, limp shake, and let it drop.

"I've heard of you. You're Ophelia's grandniece, and you run The Perfect Brew."

She gave him her best smile. "You knew my aunt?" Did he know she was a witch?

"Only by reputation."

Oh, dear. Ophelia had always been on the wild and wanton side.

The priest lifted his chin. "Your great-aunt Ophelia donated money and food to the soup kitchen. She was a good woman."

His words, though kind, failed to calm Cassie's nerves. She crossed her fingers behind her back and readied herself to do some serious protection magic. "Thank you."

"Ophelia never attended my church, mind you. I understood her to not be the religious type. What about you?" His eyes grew larger. "Do you believe in salvation, my dear?"

Cassie swallowed. "Actually, reverend." Was that the right term? "I'm here about Larry."

The priest's face paled. "Yes, I've heard the news. Poor Larry."

"A woman I met by the name of Ava told me he did janitor work here, and in exchange, you let him sleep in a back room." When the cleric didn't respond, she continued, "Is that true?"

"Yes, yes. Larry was a part of our church. We all miss him." He looked to the heavens.

Although his face remained solemn, Cassie sensed his pulse quicken. Was he sad, or was it something else? She couldn't tell. Clearly, Larry was more than just another parishioner. "Can you tell me about Larry? I find it comforting to know more about him."

Somewhere in the distance, thunder rumbled. The air

chilled, and dark clouds gathered above them. Rain was coming.

Greepsly looked up at the darkening sky and sighed. "Come inside, my dear. We'll talk in my office."

SID LET OUT a low menacing meow, as Cassie crossed the threshold of the church. Sid, with his demon blood could not go inside. Hissing, she stood as a sentinel by the door.

Cassie gave her familiar a loving look and continued into the cavernous church. She followed the priest to his office and sat across from him at his big oak desk. She wondered how many people had sat there before her and what they had come for.

"I bet he gives couples lectures about the importance of foreplay," grumbled Sid in her head.

"Ms. Black," said the priest.

"Cassie. Please, call me Cassie."

"Only if you call me, Father Jacob."

Cassie squirmed and didn't smile.

"Cassie, it is then. What is it you want to know about Larry?" He steepled his fingers on top of his desk.

"Everything, you know," she said. "Larry told people different stories about himself. No one really knows how he became homeless or if he has a family out there we should be contacting. The police don't even know his last name."

The priest frowned. "Many homeless people don't want to share their stories."

"But, I would like to contact his family. Surely a man as kind as Larry had people in his life who loved him at some point."

The priest took a deep breath and exhaled slowly. "I'm

sorry, I don't know his last name, or even if Larry was his real first name." His frown grew grimmer.

Cassie waited.

"But," the cleric continued, "In every story he told about himself, his wife and children left him. I think that's the real story about Larry. His greatest sorrow, you might say." The priest looked at his hands.

"Did you know he organized a clean-up the town?"

The priest nodded. "Yes. And he had you helping him. Yes, I knew all that. This last week he's been happier than usual."

Cassie's eyes welled with tears remembering the time she had spent with Larry. "He was a kind man and smart too. The clean-up campaign helped others just as he predicted."

"Yes, he was a good man," said Father Jacob.

Cassie sighed. 'I just don't understand his death. Who would want to kill Larry?"

"Ah, my child, none of us understands death. It is the ultimate mystery. When bad things happen to good people, it challenges our faith."

Before he could start a sermon, she repeated her own words. "Who would kill him?"

The priest shrugged. "I don't know. He got along well with most people. Occasionally, he would argue with one of the other street people, but no more so than the rest of us."

"Anyone in particular?"

Greepsly stared into space, and for a minute Cassie wondered if she had lost his attention. Should she dare try a spell on him, on holy ground? No. That would be plain stupid. She had enough trouble making a spell work on regular ground.

The priest cleared his throat. "Let's see. Harriet

Herringbone, our church organist, didn't approve of Larry staying in the church, but, I can't imagine she would physically hurt him. She prefers leveling people with her sharp tongue. There's Henry Pringle, the former janitor, who resented the fact that he lost his paying job cleaning the church, but he would never hurt anyone. And besides he got a better contract with the school board." Greepsly unfolded his fingers and tapped them on his desk. "A couple weeks ago another homeless man punched Larry. On the street, they call that guy *the psycho*. He randomly hits people thinking they are one of his demons."

Demons? That's all she needed. "Anyone else?"

"Hmm. I can't think of anyone else. Larry was well liked."

Three possible leads! Cassie stood and extended her hand. "Well, thank you, father, I appreciate our talk. I feel better. I think I just need time to grieve." She swallowed. "But if you think of anyone else who might have wanted to harm Larry, please do let me know."

He nodded. "Go in peace, my child."

As she walked down the aisle of the church, she repeated the names to herself: Harriet Herringbone, Henry Pringle and *the psycho*. With names like that, they shouldn't be hard to find. Greepsly didn't think either of them capable of murder, but harmless people had been known to do grisly things. Especially when darkness played in their head.

TEN

"Coffee, is my hot friend I was telling out about." Brianna, a barista at The Brew

Outside, sheets of rain pelted down from a low ceiling of dark clouds. Lightning zigzagged through the air in the distance. It felt to Cassie as if the whole universe lamented the loss of Larry.

"Where's Sanjay," asked Sid as they descended the church stairs and walked along the sidewalk.

"Who knows." With a quiet spell Cassie conjured an umbrella. A pink shower cap with yellow daisies appeared on her head. She groaned.

Sid snickered. "Don't you think it's odd that the big, bad warlock disappeared. He's hovered around you ever since you were poisoned, and suddenly 'poof,' he's gone."

Cassie made a face. Sid was right. Sometimes, Sanjay pretended not to be around, but whenever anything happened, like her banana peel issue, he would materialize at her side. "I guess it is a bit odd. Are you worried?"

"About the wicked warlock. Nah. He can take care of himself. I'm just curious. I think he's up to something."

Cassie tried a second time to conjure an umbrella and this time succeeded. It had purple polka dots on its see-through vinyl, but she didn't care. The rain was unrelenting and she would take whatever shelter she could.

Should she use magic to dry off her clothes? With her luck she would end up naked. To stop Sid from smirking at her, she said, "We'll ask Sanjay where he went when he reappears."

"Well Sherlock, who are we going to see next?" asked Sid.

"Kit."

"That makes sense. Do you think Sanjay has a woman on the side?"

Cassie wanted to talk about something other than the missing sorcerer. At The Brew she had heard all about his reputation with the ladies, and she didn't want to know about that part of his life. Cassie bit her lip. It had been a long time since she cared about a warlock.

Cassie exhaled noisily. "There's no point wandering all around town looking for Kit. I'll send a text to Brianna and ask her if she knows where to find him. I swear Brianna knows everything that happens in town."

The barista's reply came in one word. "Bakery."

Now that they had an umbrella, the rain stopped. Cassie vanished her brolley and ran a hand through her wet hair, spelling it to dry. It did.

They found the Mystic Main Street Bakery two blocks north of The Brew in a red brick building. Well-known for its blackberry tarts, it smelled like heaven sprinkled with cinnamon. It had a steady clientele, and today was no exception. Inside they found a mixture of locals feasting on cookies, pastries and pies. Cassie spied her friend Veronica Grunt, sitting in the corner with a business man, and headed her way. Ronnie, with her big blond hair looked larger than life, a cross between Dolly Parton and a Wall Street executive. She was the town's mayor, and a fellow witch. Just before Cassie reached the table, Ronnie's guy-friend headed for the loo. That left Cassie free to find out what she needed to know.

"Hi, Ronnie. I'm so glad to run into you." The woman stood and they hugged and kissed three times. They both sat.

Ronnie smiled. "You're looking for someone." She was a psychic, and a good one.

"Yeah," Cassie said. "A homeless guy by the name of Kit."

"Out back, in the alley," said Ronnie.

"Thanks. I just want ..."

"To ask him about Larry. I know. I hope you find the murderer."

Cassie laughed. "It's hard to surprise you. Are we on for poker next week?"

"Yup, I'm hosting."

Seeing the business man exiting the bathroom, Cassie stood. She didn't recognize him, but something about him gave her the chills. "Ronnie, do you know what you're doing? That guy hits all my alarms."

"Don't worry, Cassie. I can handle him."

No doubt she could, thought Cassie. Ronnie had a ravenous libido, and because of that her choice of men was wide and varied, which made for hilarious bedroom stories. Cassie gave her a wave and walked away.

Cassie found Kit asleep, curled up like a cat in the back doorway of the bakery. The heat of the ovens and the smell of baking leaked out from under the door. She guessed him to be in his mid-thirties. He wore jeans, a sweatshirt and a navy-blue toque. Sid swatted his leg, and he stirred.

One of his eyes opened. "What do you want?"

A life without darkness, a man I can trust..., thought Cassie, but she didn't say any of that. "I'm Cassie—"

"Everyone in town knows who you are. What do you want?" He stood up slowly, as if his joints weren't quite awake. Darkness circled his gray eyes. His Roman nose had been broken a few times and he had an open sore on his cheek that weeped with pus. He had the aura of a junkyard dog.

"I'm a friend of Larry's."

"Some good that does him now." The man looked up at the three crows sitting on the hydro line, cawing.

"I'm sorry for your loss," she said. The smell of whiskey filled her nostrils as he took a step towards her. "I'm asking around to see if I can find out what happened to him."

"Larry was like a brother to me," said Kit. "We were survivors you know. You probably heard we argued a lot. But we always made up." His left hand reached into his back pocket and pulled out a mickey. After he took a long pull on the bottle, he looked up at the black clouds skittering across the sky. "Another day in paradise," he muttered.

Sid rubbed against his legs and meowed softly.

"Hey little buddy," he said to Sid.

She jumped into his arms and nuzzled into his middle. Cassie waited. All cats have magic. "Her name is Sid," she said.

"Sid." He stroked her fur. "She's got spirit this one."

"And a big heart,' said Cassie.

"Her fur looks kinda funny, though. The way it sticks out here and there. She looks like a stray, just like me."

Cassie smiled. She could hardly tell him that the little cat he held in his arms could shift into a panther. "Do you know Larry's last name?"

"Nope."

Sid purred, a rumbling sound that reverberated in the air around them. Normally she kept it toned down, but on this occasion, she let it loose.

"Well hell," said the man. "This cat has moxy."

"You're Kit. Right?"

"Yeah." He made eye contact with Sid.

"What did you and Larry fight about last week?" She waited for an answer, and when none came, she thought maybe he didn't hear her.

Sid nipped his finger.

"Ouch. Hey little girl, I'll answer." He shrugged. "Larry borrowed my shopping cart and didn't return it. I lost it, and punched him. I have anger issues, you know." He stroked Sid. "Anyway, the next day he got me another one and I apologized. No big deal."

"Can you think of anyone who would want to hurt Larry?"

"Everyone liked Larry." Kit sounded jealous.

"Until someone didn't," said Cassie.

"I figure he was in the wrong place at the wrong time. Saw something he shouldn't have. Or maybe it was one of the creeps who hates the homeless."

"But you have no idea who actually did it?"

Kit shook his head and became enraptured by Sid's purrs. "If I knew who did it, I'd deal with them." He stopped and tilted his head. "There is Ava."

"What about Ava?"

"She talks too much. Sometimes, that got on Larry's nerves. Maybe he said something to her and she blew him away. She's a strange one."

"Hard to imagine. Anyone else?"

His lips pursed as if he wanted to say something, but wasn't sure he should. Sid purred louder.

"There's that new dude in town. A suit from the city."

Cassie waited.

Kit sniffed. "I warned Larry. That guy feels mean, you know."

"Do you know his name?"

"Uh, let me think. He wears suits and uses stuff in his hair. Smells of cologne."

Cassie held her breath. The image of the guy sitting with Ronnie flashed into her mind.

"His name reminded me of a tree."

A tree! "Cedar? Fir? Hemlock? Weeping Willow?"

"That's it. His name was Reaper."

"Weeper Reaper. Got it," said Cassie.

Cassie's cell rang with a text from Sanjay. "Need to see you now. Meet me at The Brew."

ELEVEN

"For the love of coffee!" ~ Ophelia

Cassie and Sid rushed back to The Perfect Brew, but Sanjay hadn't arrived. She sent him a text. No response. Warlocks!

Cassie ordered a coffee and waited. Then she ordered a late lunch. An hour later a text came in from Sanjay, "Sorry, got delayed. Will talk soon."

An irate supplier of toilet paper called The Brew demanding payment. Cassie spent the rest of her afternoon wading through bills in her office. Ophelia had made her grand vision of a supernatural haven come alive, but she sucked at book keeping. On paper Cassie had inherited a financial mess.

Ophelia ordered the best of everything, but she never paid anyone. Cassie wondered if her great-aunt ever paid a bill in her life. Maybe she charmed her suppliers? Whatever. Cassie needed to fix things. She wanted the business accounts of The Brew settled, so that if anyone came snooping around they would find the paper work in order.

The last thing she needed was for someone like Gavin to find out bills had not been paid on time. After four hours of paper-hell, she ate a sandwich by the fire in the main room with Stormy. When the café closed she headed upstairs.

In her apartment she caught up with her friends and family on social media. An hour later she curled up on the sofa to read. She would face more bills and Sanjay the next day.

But she couldn't read. One task nagged at her between every sentence. She needed to talk to Alessandro.

Her call was picked up after one ring. "Rare Antiquities, International. How may I help you?" Cassie recognized Jordan's low baritone voice. He was Alessandro's dayman.

"It's me," she said.

"How nice to hear your voice, Cassie."

Sarcasm? Great! What were they saying about her in her old neighborhood? Did she even want to know? Cassie scrunched her face. "I want to leave a message for Alessandro."

"Okay."

"Please, tell him ..." She paused. Her mind went blank. Although she had thought about her message all day long, her mouth couldn't seem to move.

"Cassie, are you still there?"

"Yeah. Yeah." Of course, she was there. Where else would she be?

"Alessandro wishes to speak to you." No sarcasm now, she noted.

Jordan must have buzzed his coffin. That wasn't part of her plan. They used the buzzer system for extreme emergencies, like vampire wars. Not for her.

Now what? Eye of Newt! She had talked herself into leaving a message, not to listening to Alessandro's charming vampire voice calling her back to him. His drop-dead sexy tone would remind her of things she didn't want to think about.

Sid, who lay at her side, whipped her tail up and down.

Cassie sighed. Her heart filled with conflicting emotions. Some good, some bad and some supremely naughty. Alessandro had the deep voice of a seasoned warrior, a man who had seen much of life and death, and of a lover never to be forgotten. Could she handle him? She braced herself.

"Cassie, my love, how nice of you to call." His words hit her even harder than she expected. They had left so much unsaid and whether she liked it or not, she still had feelings for him.

Sid purred and clawed at the pillow.

Cassie looked at the ceiling. "Alessandro, I may be in trouble."

"Tell me."

"Someone shot Larry, a middle-aged, homeless man who lives in Mystic Keep, the town I'm staying in. I cared about him."

"I'm sorry."

"It gets worse. In his hand he held a note that read, 'BLACK WITCH BEWARE,' in capitals."

"I don't like the sound of that," he said.

She took a deep breath. "Written in blood."

"Cassie, come home to me."

"I can't. I need to protect the portal."

"Screw the portal. It has existed for centuries without you, and it can continue to exist without you. If some darkness seeps in, so be it. I'll protect you."

"I can't risk it."

"Cassie, give me, give us, another chance. Lola means nothing to me."

Lola! He would bring up Lola, the thin, bright-eyed, red-haired, young vampire he recently sired. She had been the final straw in their five-year relationship. "It didn't look like *nothing* when I walked in on the two of you going at it like fevered animals." Had she stayed in Amsterdam, they might have patched things up, but her call to Mystic Keep had given her time to think about their relationship. Would he always be siring young women? Perhaps her family had been right about Alessandro, the whole time.

Cassie exhaled slowly. "It's not about her. I truly *have* to be here. I feel it in my bones. This is where I'm meant to be right now."

"I don't like you being so far from me. It is hard to protect you."

"I can protect myself." Sort of. Who was she kidding? She could barely boil water with her spells. "I need to know what I'm up against. That's why I'm calling you for help. Is there a vamp war happening?"

He chuckled. "Do you think a vampire would leave a note?"

"I guess not. So you don't think a vampire is involved."

"Not likely. While we enjoy threatening people, writing notes is not what we do. As you know, I like to show fang, and if I'm really angry, I hiss."

Sid's purrs grew louder.

Show fang! Cassie rolled her eyes. "The fact that they used blood to write the note made me wonder if a vampire was involved."

"Let's cut to the blood," he laughed at his own joke. "You wonder if one of my enemies is harassing you to get to me. I understand. But, if someone wanted to hurt me, they would grab you and hold you hostage. They would play with you like a cat plays with a mouse, and that would torture me. That's what vampires do. Taunting you with a note is too passive a threat."

"Hostage?" Of a vampire! Now that was something she didn't want to think about. How many times had her father warned her that she shouldn't get involved with a ghoul?

"My dear, fear not. I highly doubt your note has anything to do with my world, but trust me, I will find out."

"Thank you."

"Anything else I can help you with?"

"That's it."

"You don't want to talk about us? Maybe have a bit of phone sex?"

"Alessandro, my time with you has been ..."

"Has been?" His voice rose.

"Alessandro, you have to understand. This town. The portal. The café. All of it. It's changing me. I'm not the same person."

"Cassie, no one changes that quickly. Trust me. I've been around for two centuries. I know all about character change. We need to spend time together. Get reacquainted. Talk over our differences." He made a guttural sound only aroused vampires make. "Let me hold you, my love."

Sid rolled over so many times she fell off the edge of the bed.

"Not now, my sweet dark soul. Maybe, I can steal away for a few days after this is all over, and we can talk about things."

Silence hung for a second. "Did Jane arrive, yet?

Jane? "My sister?"

"Two days ago, she came to me asking for you. She thought I was protecting you for some reason. And, she said, she had had something important to tell you. Something about a dream. I told her you were having an American adventure in a small town with a New Age name." He chuckled.

A shudder ran through Cassie's system. Jane had premonitions. Big premonitions. It could have something to do with the blood note. "Did you tell her to come to Mystic Keep?"

"She flew out yesterday."

Cassie used her fingers to calculate the hours it would take her to fly into Seattle, rent a car and drive to Mystic Keep. She should arrive ...

The wards rang. An intruder had attempted to cross the front door.

"Gotta go," said Cassie.

"Wait. No sex? I so want to stroke your –"

"I'll be in touch."

Alessandro growled. "Till next time, my love."

TWELVE

"Coffee is my love language." ∼ anon

Cassie ran down the stairs to the front door of the café with Sid at her heels. Could it really be Jane? Why didn't she text first? Why didn't she calm the wards? Why? She opened the door.

There stood Detective Gavin MacGregor, back lit by the glow of the streetlights. His rumpled hair, and five-o'clock shadow looked good on him. "Cassie, I'm sorry to disturb you," he said. His eyes widened.

Oh, dandelion poop. She glanced down at her night-gown, which was actually a tee-shirt she once borrowed from the vampire and never returned. She put a hand on her hip. "Let me guess. You want a cup of coffee?"

His face flushed. "No, I came to talk to you. You see, the night clerk at the station called me. A young woman, who claims to be your sister is in the drunk tank. I thought you should know, in case she really is your sister. I tried your cell phone, but your line was busy, so I thought I'd come over."

His eyes glanced over her body once more before they settled on the ground.

"Is her name Jane Black?" Cassie said.

"That's the name she used." He pulled out his notebook and read from it. "Jane Zenia Black."

"And the station called you."

His face turned even redder. She loved how he couldn't control his complexion.

Gavin cleared his throat. "Now that we have a murder on our hands, I've asked the desk to inform me of anything unusual. Apparently, your sister is unusual."

Cassie smiled. "You could say that. Many have."

He squinted.

"I can see you haven't met her yet."

"I thought I'd take you with me."

"Give me a couple minutes." Cassie closed the door, spelled a full set of clothes onto her body, waited a few minutes and opened the door.

GAVIN HATED LYING. It went against his personal code, and his father taught him a man's code was the only thing he actually owned. You lose your code, you got nothing, he would say.

And yet Gavin had lied to Cassie. He had asked the office staff to contact him whenever anything came up that had to do with her. His gut told him she was trouble, but his heart wasn't sure. He needed to know, once and for all, if she was at the bottom of all the strange things happening in town. Like the report of a woman floating down Main Street, or the wolf that walked on two legs. If he told his superiors about all of this weird stuff in Mystic Keep, they would ask him what he put in his morning coffee. He sensed the beautiful, green-eyed Cassie, the woman he fantasized about, was at the center of it all.

When the door re-opened, and he smelled her wild-flower perfume Gavin reminded himself that this was a business outing.

Sid followed them and jumped into the back of Gavin's sports car, where his dog Marlowe greeted him with a snarl. The cat reached out with a paw and smacked the retriever on the nose. Marlow whined.

Cassie took Gavin's hand. "They're just being animals. Ignore them." As he inhaled her scent and felt the softness of her skin, suddenly it didn't matter that his dog hated her cat.

"Marlowe, behave," he commanded. The dog growled. Sid lifted her head into the evening breeze. They drove to the station.

"EVERY FAMILY HAS A JANE," Cassie said as he drove. How could she explain her baby sister, the wildest of all the wild Black witches? "You know the one who keeps the party going." Wanting to describe her in terms Gavin could understand she continued, "She's the youngest in a family of six girls. Her real name is Scorpius, but she changed it to Jane when she turned five and got hooked on Tarzan."

"That's a lot of kids."

"My mom loved kids."

"All the same dad?"

"No, Jane's dad, Gren, is not my dad." Thank the good universe. Grendor, was a wizard best known for dabbling in ancient and complicated magic, which could be enter-taining some days and terrifying others. The last time Cassie saw him, he created a replica Hobbit world in a new dimension, calling it a piece of living art. It was more an act of hubris. Grendor enjoyed playing god to a new genre of people created from android-human-hybrids. She shuddered at the memory. Her mom threw him out of the house. The wizard needed boundaries.

Before she could say more they arrived at the police station. That was the thing about their small town. Even without magic, you arrived everywhere quickly.

Jane, dressed in blue jeans, a tight, black cotton halter top and flip flops looked ready for a California beach. A wide, mischievous smile, lit up her freckled face. Her bright-red curls tumbled over her bare shoulders. Large china-blue eyes dominated her face. "Look who's come to save me!" she said.

Cassie laughed at that idea. "What in the name of goodness did you do to land yourself in jail?" A mundane human jail, no less.

"It wasn't my fault."

"It never is." Cassie wanted to remain calm, but her pulse raced. Dealing with twenty-year old Jane brought out the worst in her. She fisted her hands and felt her nails dig into her palms.

Jane tossed her hair behind her shoulders. "There were these two biker guys. See."

"Two?" Cassie couldn't help but smile as the picture began to form in her mind.

"They were big, Cassie."

"Uh, huh. And where did you meet these men?"

"Big and mean. They didn't treat me well, and I could tell their intentions were not honorable."

How many times had she heard this story? It usually ended with bloody details. Forget Jane's innocent baby-blues welling with stage tears. She had a mean streak in her.

Luckily, for most of the world, it only showed when she crossed paths with evil doers. Feeling Gavin's eyes on her, Cassie played her part, "Are you all right, honey?"

"I'm fine. Well, a little stiff. But nothing a hot bath won't fix."

Eye of Newt. She wants to come home with me. "I'm not sure they have soaker tubs in the clinker."

Jane snickered "Aren't you going to get me out of here?"

Cassie turned to Gavin. "Officer, what's she in for?"

"The patrol men said she caused a ruckus." His eyes were glued on Jane's. No doubt she charmed him with her wild-beauty, and her magic.

Jane smiled.

Cassie waved her hand in front of Gavin's face and snapped her fingers. "Dice mihi," Tell me.

Gavin blinked. "They said she threw things around. Big things, like cars and a fire hydrant."

Cassie glared at Jane. "Seriously? In front of bystanders?'

Jane shrugged. "The bikers made me mad."

Cassie rolled her eyes. "Gavin, how much damage was there?"

He blinked twice. Darn it, her spell was weakening.

Jane spoke up. "Don't worry, Cassie. I fixed it all." She tilted her head. "But not before a truck driver saw me. He called the police and they didn't know what to do with me so they brought me here, and when they found out my last name was Black, they called in this guy. He's hot. Is he available?"

"Hands off." That came out too quickly. "He's a widow."

Jane winked. "Gotcha." She unlocked the cell door with a

wave of her hand. "I could really do with a bath." With another wave of her hand Gavin's face became expressionless.

He put a hand to his forehead. "You are free to go, Ms. Black. I hope you like our town."

"Oh, I will, detective." Jane linked her arm in her sisters and strutted out.

As soon as they were outside, Jane's familiar, an overweight, orange tabby called Vixen, joined them. Known in the family to be the world's best cuddle-monster, he was the most affectionate cat Cassie had ever met.

Cassie looked to the heavens. How many things could she juggle before she broke. "Jane, I'm not sure you'll like it here."

Vixen leaped onto Sid's back and a friendly tussle ensued.

"I had to find out what this town has that keeps you away from the yummy Alessandro. I think I may have just met him. Am I right?"

Sanjay appeared outside the door of the police station as they exited. "Good evening, ladies." His marmalade eyes blazed with power. His familiar, Peregrine, sat on his shoulder looking at the cats making clicking sounds.

Jane grinned at her sister. "I see your life is complicated."

Cassie elbowed her. "If you don't want me to put slugs in your bed tonight, button up."

Jane extended her hand to Sanjay. "I am Jane Black, daughter of ..."

Sanjay stopped her genetic tale by taking her hand and kissed the inside of her wrist, a sign of trust usually reserved for a closed circle of family and loyal friends. "Your reputation, little one, precedes you." He stared into her eyes, "But

I must say you are even more beautiful than I had been told."

"Oh, my." Jane's cheeks reddened.

Sanjay didn't let go of her hand. "But, you must behave in our town," he said with authority, "or my little one, you will answer to me.'

"And me," Cassie added, as a surge of joy rose inside her. No one, absolutely no one, ever tried to control Jane Not even Gren. She had a slippery, sly way of getting past everyone, but Sanjay seemed to have her enthralled with his charm.

Jane tried to pull her hand away from Sanjay, but couldn't. She stomped her foot, swore, hexed in Latin, hexed in Swahili and stomped her foot again. A kaleidoscope of colorful mist rose around them, but Sanjay held on. He snapped his fingers and a cloaking spell covered them as snuggly as a cotton duvet. No strangers would see their power struggle.

Cassie bit her lip to stop herself from giggling.

Jane gave in, and the spells dissipated. Sanjay let go of her hand and she rubbed it. "Do you know who my father is?" she said to him.

"Yes, and I do not care." His tiger eyes turned a vibrant shade of orange and power flowed from every pore of his skin.

She glared at him. "We'll see about that!" She walked off ten meters.

Cassie mouthed 'Thank you,' to Sanjay. He shrugged. "I have a little sister, too."

Jane turned around, "Where are we going?"

Gavin came out of the building looking as if he had just woken from a dream. "Cassie, Sanjay, Jane ..."

"I'm taking my sister home," Cassie explained. "Thank you for bringing me to her. You've been a great help."

"Ah, okay." He scratched the stubble on his cheek. "Glad I could help."

Cassie took one of Jane's arms. Sanjay took the other. "Walk this way," he said in a low voice. Cassie could feel Gavin's eyes on their backs.

"I think Gavin's catching on," Cassie said.

Sanjay groaned. "He suspects, but he knows nothing for sure. Let's keep it that way."

"He's a good detective. It's only a matter of time. What will we do if he figures it out?" said Cassie

"That's the least of our problems." Sanjay increased their pace.

Cassie swallowed. She hated it when he said things like that. "Dare I ask?"

"First, things first. Why is Jane here?"

The red head lifted her chin. "Are you commanding me to answer?"

He growled.

"All right. All right. I had a vision."

"Eye of Newt," said Cassie. "Jane is the seer in our generation of Black witches. When she has a vision, it's rarely wrong."

"Out with it," demanded Sanjay. "What did you see?"

The moon peaked out from behind a cloud, lighting their path. In the distance an owl hooted. Cassie held her breath. In her experience premonitions were rarely good.

Jane narrowed her eyes at him. "I'm not sure I want to share it with you, warlock."

"I'll send you to my dungeon and make you listen to really bad music if you don't."

She laughed, and turned to Cassie. "I like him."

Of course, you do. "Charm should be his second name," she said out loud.

"Jane, you're stalling," he said.

The young witch pursed her lips. "There is danger There is magic. There is love."

"Goddess, give me a broom," said Sanjay. "Get on with it."

"Before the next full moon, Cassie will be visited by darkness."

Cassie shuddered. Jane wouldn't tell Sanjay the whole vision, but what she said was more than enough to give her nightmares. "So," she said to her sister, as they walked in step, "you came to protect me."

"I came to warn you. You must be careful."

Sanjay laughed. "That would be a good warning for Cassie on any day. Just today she was attacked by a wanton banana peel. Please, tell us more."

Jane's eyes lit with magic and she recited an incantation beneath her breath. The air stirred around them, swirling in a vortex. The sound of wolves baying in the distance became louder.

Sanjay's eyes widened.

The wind died down and Jane spoke. "I will share my vision only with Cassie, and only when I am ready. Be careful, warlock, or I will spell you to my father's dungeon, and you don't want to know what he does to men I send there."

Sanjay knowing full well who her father was, smirked. "I am impressed. I will trust that Cassie will let me know the details, I need to know to keep us all safe."

"Of course." Cassie lied. After all, words spoken between Black sisters were always kept secret.

They walked a few more steps in silence, under the moonlight, taking in each other's measure.

Cassie turned to Sanjay. "So, what's more dangerous than the local copper knowing I'm a witch?"

His right brow rose. "Someone is knocking on our door."

"Door?" said Jane. "What door? What are you guys talking about?"

"Our portal door," grumbled Cassie.

"Cool," said Jane.

THIRTEEN

"Ever have one of those mornings, Ethel, where ya just
wanna fill the sink with coffee & stick your head in?"
~ *Lucille Ball, I Love Lucy*

Cassie, Jane and Sanjay walked through the front door of
The Perfect Brew as the antique clock struck midnight.
Their familiars followed. A miniature raven came out of the
time-piece and cawed twelve times. Jane clapped her hands
and did a dance. "I love this place," she said. She ran her
hands over the odd collection of chairs. Sanjay spelled the
front door closed and locked before he followed Cassie's
lead to the back staircase.

Once upstairs, Cassie left Sanjay in the living room
with a bottle of beer, and gave Jane the grand tour of the
apartment. Jane squealed when she saw the guest room, and
bounced on the bed. Taking that as a good sign, Cassie left
her and her familiar to settle in, and headed reluctantly to
the warlock in the living room.

Talk about being caught between a hex and a spell! If
she stayed in the guest room, her sister would tell her more

about the vision of darkness threatening her future. If she went into the living room, Sanjay would tell her something equally bad about the portal. She could feel it in her bones. When the forces of darkness knew your broom number, there was no place to hide. So, she took a long bathroom break and contemplated the texture of the paint on the ceiling.

When she entered the living room fifteen minutes later, Sanjay poured two glasses of local red wine for them. She took a glass and sat opposite him in a comfortable wing chair. Peregrine flew through a magical portal and settled on the mantelpiece, while Sid snored at the warlock's feet.

After a long sip of wine, Cassie said, "What's bothering you?"

"Where do I start?" he said.

She took another sip. "Will our lives ever calm down?"

"Depends. How many sisters do you have?"

She laughed. "Good point." She took a gulp. Had he charmed her drink? That was always a possibility. "So, what's your plan?"

"First, tell me how your Vamp-angle is going."

"It's been covered."

His golden eyes deepened to the color of a sunset on a warm September evening. "Cassie, I trust you. You are one of the sincerest women, I have ever met. It's the rest of the universe I'm worried about."

A compliment from a rogue warlock. Hmph. Over the rim of her wine glass she took measure of the sorcerer who she had hated on first sight. His bad boy swagger had set off all her alarms. But much had happened in three months, and she now recognized the man beneath the warlock cloak was true of heart and despite all the boundaries she set between them, was becoming a good friend.

Sid, knowing her thoughts, purred.

Yeah, the change in her feelings created problems. Sanjay was no ordinary warlock. He had to be the sexiest man alive. His face, all sharp angles and seductive shadows, would fit nicely or a Greek sculpture. His eyes blazed with latent power, and his body was made perfect for play. She bit her lip. "Did you charm my drink?"

"No, Cassie. I told you before, and I'll tell you again. I will not charm you, in any way, without your consent." His grin warmed the room.

"Oh, strike me bewitched, you are hard to resist, Sanjay Kahn."

"I suggest you stop trying."

"I can't. We can't. Things would be way too compli- cated if we were to act on my thoughts." The sound of the bath water running in the guest room reminded her that they weren't alone.

He sighed. "Someday, Cassie. Someday I hope you will act on your feelings and not your thoughts."

Sid purred louder.

Cassie shook herself. She needed to be serious. A man was dead. Things weren't right in the Keep. Her sister was having visions. It was no time to play innuendo with a warlock. "So, tell me about our visitor."

"Tell me about your vamp?"

My vamp? Did he know something? "I told you, I'm handling it."

"You said that, but vamps aren't easy to handle. There's the matter of their teeth for one. Can you handle the blood- suckers on your own? I wonder." His lips pressed into a flat line. When she didn't respond, he continued. "Okay, back to our problem. The knocking on the portal door started earlier this evening. When we go into the attic, you'll hear it. It has the somber sound of wind chimes, and a steady beat."

"Great, a persistent knocker." She licked her lips. The wine tasted delicious. "We need a peep hole on that door."

Sanjay toasted her. "My thoughts exactly."

"Can we do it?"

"I thought we'd finish our wine first, but if you insist." He snapped his fingers and a spiralling orange vortex of energy appeared in the room.

Leaving Jane singing in her bath, they walked into it and arrived in Ophelia's magic attic chamber. The knocking sound echoed in the room. Sid hissed.

Cassie touched Ophelia's rose-colored crystal ball, which sat on the desk next to her grimoire. It mumbled to Cassie, but she had no idea how to communicate with it. She failed scrying at the academy. "I wish I could use this thing," she said.

Sanjay raised a brow. "Uh-huh." With a click of his fingers another crystal ball appeared, swirling with purple energy. They gathered around it. Sanjay cast a spell "Voco super terram et maria in caelum ... crystal pila ad me quid tu vides." I call on the earth, the sky and the seas. Crystal ball tell me what you see.

The globe turned bright red as the power within it continued to swirl. The warlock put his hand above it and Cassie added hers on top of his. She felt the familiar jolt of their combined power. The red energy turned pink and then a misty-blue. Within the cloud of color she could see the portal door.

"Well done," said Sanjay. He gave her an appreciative glance. It seemed she wasn't the only one reappraising the other. The pounding continued. "Should we open the portal door from here?" asked Cassie.

Sensing danger Sid shifted into her panther form and put her paws on the table. Peregrine landed on her back.

A dark sense of foreboding settled on Cassie's shoulders. It felt like the weight of the world. "Whoever is pounding on our door may be in trouble," she said.

"Or," said Sanjay, "they may be the trouble."

Sid gave a menacing growl. The knocking stopped.

"Huh," said Cassie. "Do you think our visitor heard Sid?"

The warlock's jaw line firmed. "I am Sanjay Kahn, son of Adrian Kahn. I command you to identify yourself."

Silence.

Sid snarled. Cassie had forgotten how large her familiar's teeth could grow.

"I need help," said a tiny voice.

"I told you so," Cassie whispered. "They're in trouble. It's a big universe out there and we should be, a safe haven to all. We swore an oath to do just that. We have to help them."

Sanjay's eyes narrowed as he peered into the crystal ball. "Who are you?"

"I am ..."

Silence.

Sanjay looked at Cassie. Cassie looked at Sid. "Can you smell them?" she asked her familiar.

"They've gone," the demon panther said as she shifted back into her housecat form with tufts of black fur sticking out here and there all over her body.

"Could you tell what she was?" asked Sanjay.

"Not human. It smelled like a heap of decomposing vegetation and rotting meat, but I wonder if they used that stench to hide their identity."

"Great," said Cassie. "We have a visitor from an

unknown dimension who smells like putrefied matter. I'll take that as a bad sign." Even her bones felt weary. Maybe, she had had too much to drink.

"Let's strengthen the wards," said Sanjay. It was something they did regularly. Their hands touched. Cassie felt the jolt. They chanted. Magic happened.

Cassie wasn't sure she would ever get used to their combined power, or their unusual bond. As they chanted their spells rhythmically, a cool breeze swirled around them and the wards protecting The Perfect Brew and the town strengthened.

When they were done, Sanjay escorted her back to her living room and gave her a chaste kiss on the cheek. "I will see what the Warlock Brotherhood can tell me about our visitor."

"And, I'll talk with Jane about her vision."

FOURTEEN

"Life happens. Coffee helps."
~ Coffee Meme, Soul and Wine, FB

As soon as the warlock left, Jane came out of the guest room wrapped in a towel. "Where did he go? she asked.

Cassie sat on the sofa stroking Sid. "He has warlock business to tend to."

"Hmm. I'd love to be his business."

"Jane."

"What? I can look, can't I?" She paused. "Or is he spoken for too? As in two hot guys and one witch?" She wiggled her nose.

Cassie winced. "No, it's not like that. He's too old for you. And, he's a warlock. The cop is too old for you and he's a mundane. Neither are right for you."

"It's my experience that warlocks are fun to play with. Mother married three."

"Jane "

"They are rumored to be expert lovers."

"Jane."

"They never tire and they have magic potions that ..."

"Jane!"

"Okay, I'll give it a rest." She rubbed her long, wet hair with the towel. "But, I have to say I noticed how he looked at you. Kind of like how a starving man looks at a steak."

"Jane."

"What I'd give to have any man look at me like that." Jane batted her eyelashes. "Let alone a delicious warlock!"

"Enough, all ready. Tell me about your vision."

Jane tossed her wet towel into the air and snapped her fingers. It flew back to the bathroom, folding itself on the way. She snapped her fingers a second time and shimmied her body until it was clothed in soft cotton pajamas with pink unicorns. After a glance at herself, she sat down on the wing chair opposite Cassie. Vixen jumped on her lap. "As I said, I had a vision."

How many times had Cassie heard Jane start a story with, 'I had a vision.' Rarely had she liked the tales. "Okay, hit me. What happened in your vision?"

"You were riding on a brightly painted horse in a calliope, going up and down, smiling like I've never seen you smile before. You looked as if your life had come together and you knew who you were and what you wanted. You looked on top of the world." Jane took a deep breath and let it out slowly.

Cassie waited.

"A black cloud appeared at the edge of my vision. It chased you on your stallion. Sid sat on your shoulder. Around and around it went, inching closer and closer to you. But you continued to smile, as if you were unaware."

Well, at least I smiled, thought Cassie.

"The music changed to a dirge as the shadow wrapped itself around you."

"What did I do?"

"You tried to scream, but no sound came out of your mouth. Sid jumped to the ground and ran for help."

Sid purred and rolled on her back punching the air with her paws.

"The cloud squeezed tighter around your body, and it laughed, like the bad guy in a really bad movie."

Cassie swallowed.

"Wait, it's not over. A warlock appeared, but you were already gone. I now recognize the warlock as Sanjay."

"Jane, have you been taking drugs?"

She glared at Cassie. "No. I'm dead serious. I'm not sure what all the symbolism in my prophecy means, but I do know that you are in grave danger. So, of course, I came."

Cassie got up and gave Jane a big hug.

She swiped at a tear trickling down her cheek. "Thank you," she said. Her sister may be young, but she was a gifted witch. Cassie could not be more proud of her, or more terrified.

Jane nodded. "Who is your enemy, Cassie? Tell me that. Let me at them. I'll make them go away."

Cassie laughed. "I wish life was that simple. I'm not sure who the black cloud is, but I don't doubt they exist." Where should she start her story? "You see I'm not just running a coffee house, I'm also protecting the portal beneath it. That's the portal Sanjay was talking about."

"You're a guardian?" Jane's blue eyes grew large and sparkled with delight. "I never imagined you ..."

"With Sanjay."

"Now that is interesting."

"Interesting is one word for it. When I first came, the wards had been weakened and something came through. That could be the black cloud in your vision."

"But it hasn't done anything to you. Right?"

Cassie grimaced. "There's been two evil events. Ophelia was murdered and then someone poisoned me. I'm not sure who is behind it all."

"Murder! Poison!" Her sister put her hand to her mouth. "You didn't tell the family."

"I planned to as soon as I knew more. There's no point worrying people."

"That's why I had the vision. The goddess wanted to help you."

"And she chose the perfect witch," said Cassie.

Jane paced the floor. "Someone in town must have seen something."

"You can't spell the entire town."

A wand appeared in her sister's hand. "Why not?"

"This is a haven for supernaturals. We want to keep our existence hidden from the regular folk."

"I'm guessing the cop already thinks you're a witch."

"Possibly." Cassie nodded. "But he isn't sure. We need to keep a low profile, which means we need to do our sleuthing, as if we were normal women."

"You're no fun."

Cassie laughed. "I'm not supposed to be. I'm your big sister."

Jane grinned. "So, tell me about the man in blue."

"The cop? I met him the day I arrived, when I ran into his beloved sport's car." Cassie rolled her eyes. "I thought he'd never forgive me."

Jane laughed. "Not a great way to get to know a guy."

Cassie told Jane all about Ophelia's death and funeral.

She also told her about the sea-witch's explanation of why she and Sanjay had been chosen to protect the portal, though she still felt it more of a curse than an honor. Finally, she told Jane about Larry. "So, with all these things happening," Cassie said, "I keep running into Gavin."

"No wonder he's growing suspicious of you," said Jane.

"Yeah yeah. And I also solved a mundane murder for him. But that's no concern now."

"Uh-huh. There are worse people to run into." Jane gave her a crooked smile.

"True," Jane smiled back. "I don't like him thinking I'm bad."

"Can you blame him?" Jane snickered.

"No. And get this, when Larry died he was holding a note in his hand, that implicates me.."

"No way." Jane's blue eyes widened.

"It read, 'BEWARE BLACK WITCH,' and it was written in blood."

"Good grief!"

"I keep crossing paths with the lawman."

Jane smirked. "Is that all you cross?"

Cassie hesitated. "Well ..."

"Ooooh. You gotta tell me."

"We did have one kiss, but it meant nothing." Though she could still taste it on her lips. "We're not romantically involved." He wasn't for her. "He's a widower, a mundane and a cop. What would mother say? "And before you tell me to just have fun with him, I have to add he's a grieving husband."

"Was it good? The kiss."

Jane had looked right through her. "Oh, yeah," Cassie admitted. "It was a whopper. All passion and promise."

"Ooooh." Jane sat up again. "And compared to Sanjay?"

"I wouldn't know," Cassie said stiffly. "We've never kissed."

"Never?"

"Never."

"You will."

FIFTEEN

"Espresso is a miracle of chemistry in a cup." ~ Andrea Illy

Sanjay stood on the balcony of his turret watching the surf pound the rocky cliff below. The almost full moon peaked between the low cloud cover, revealing a dark and angry sea. The spray from the surf rose high up the rock face, upon which his house perched. He could smell the approaching storm. And worse, in his bones, he could feel darkness rising

He didn't know where it would come from or when it would arrive, but he had no doubt the evil that had leaked into their world was about to reveal itself again. A chill crawled through his veins.

A flaming note flew through the air, and hovered in front of his face. He reached out and grabbed it, hoping it was good news from The Warlock Brotherhood.

'You are summoned,' it read.

Peregrine flew to his shoulder.

The Brotherhood considered themselves above others, and so they wasted no words in their correspondence. This he already knew. But three words! Three! They gave him no indication as to whether his letter had been welcomed, or not. They should be happy that a warlock of my power and pedigree wants to rejoin the ranks.

"But...," said his falcon in his head.

"Yeah," Sanjay replied out loud. "But there are those who don't want me in the group." He dropped the ashes of the note into the sea. "Screw them. I will go." If he wanted to protect Mystic Keep and Cassie, he had no choice.

AN HOUR LATER, after meditating and preparing himself with a magical elixir, he created a portal to Castle Brock in the Highlands of Scotland, the home of the Brotherhood. He flew through the magical worm in his raven form with Peregrine as his shadow. As Sanjay landed on the marble floor in the middle of the council room he folded his majestic wings, and in a whirlwind of magic transformed back into his human shape. Dressed to impress, he wore black pants, a black dress shirt, and expensive shoes. He wore his family ring and a crystal pendant for protection.

It had been twenty years since he had last attended a council meeting, but by all appearances nothing had changed. A hundred people sat in their designated places. The inner circle of thirteen were in tall chairs carved out of ancient wood, cloaked in spells. Behind them sat a middle circle of warlocks in folding chairs who attended meetings but were not part of the inner circle. They had no vote. And behind that group stood bystanders, not all warlocks, but all magical in some sense. Sanjay looked up. An enormous crystal chandelier hung from the center of a coffered, mahogany ceiling spreading a rainbow of light in all directions. The pungent smell of old magic and warlocks hung in the air.

A gong sounded, announcing his arrival, and quieting the crowd.

As Peregrine settled on Sanjay's shoulder, the warlock looked around once more nodding at members he recognized. It had been twenty years since he stood before them. Many were the same, but some had changed. A position in this circle was hereditary. In his family's chair sat his father, Arjun Khan, a stately older version of himself with black hair and orange eyes. He spoke first.

"My son, I welcome you to the court of the Brotherhood."

Sanjay bowed. "I am honored to be summoned."

The room became deathly quiet. He straightened. "For anyone in the audience who does not know me, let me introduce myself. I am Sanjay Kahn, son of Arjun Khan, the ninth son of the ninth son of the great Arjun Sanjay Khan. I am a warlock and though I have been rogue for the last twenty years, I am loyal to the Brotherhood." He tipped his head in respect.

A man from the other side of the circle spoke. "Sanjay Khan, be honest. You are loyal to no one but yourself. Always have been. Now that you have run into some trouble you've come running back to us. Why should we take you in?" His dark resonant voice echoed in the great hall.

Sanjay turned to face the speaker. Thomas Brackenfeld. Of course. He was one of the oldest in the group, and known for his cruelty. He wore a scar across his left cheek from Sanjay's magic. Sanjay nodded to him in respect.

They had butted magic twenty years ago when Sanjay helped Brackenfeld's wife, Arianna, escape from his beatings. The warlocks had fought viciously. The older sorcerer looked no different than he had all those years ago. Standing nearly seven feet tall he loomed over his peers and cast a shadow where ever he roamed. He wore all black: a tightly knit cashmere sweater, leather pants and tall boots. His cape, made of dragon skin, glowed with deep magic.

Recognizing the deep hatred in the older warlock's eyes, Sanjay's hand tingled for his wand. But he didn't reach for it. Instead, Sanjay bowed. "I respect your hatred for me Brackenfeld, and we could debate until the dragons return whether it's justified, but I must remind you, you are not the sole voice of the Brotherhood."

Chatter grew in the outer throng. The middle circle drew their wands for protection. The only ones who remained quiet were those sitting in the inner-circle. Sanjay regained his height and looked around, taking the measure of the room.

"Let me tell you about my situation," Sanjay said.

"Yada, yada, yada." Brackenfeld's voice boomed. "You wrote us all about it. Your note read like a woman's romance novel. You found yourself caught up in a situation you can't handle on your own, and you've come running to us to bail you out. You're a disgrace to our kind."

"You're right," answered Sanjay. "I am facing danger, and I'm not sure I can handle it on my own. The Brotherhood taught me that one should never allow pride to stand in your way. I know this dark force could be stronger than me, and while I'm prepared to take it on and lose my own life if necessary, I'm not prepared to let it hurt others. I come to ask for your help to protect them."

"I don't understand how you became a guardian of an inter-dimensional portal." Lester Grenchen spoke from the inner-circle.

Sanjay smiled. "I don't understand either."

"You say you are chosen." Brackenfeld's voice dripped with sarcasm. "What force on this earth would choose ..."

Before he finished speaking a streak of white lightening zapped across the great hall. The warlocks stood and held their wands to the sky in defence.

But all was still.

"Brackenfeld, you were saying?" asked Arjun Khan who took his seat first, as if the crackle of lightning was a usual occurrence when his son arrived.

The rest of the room sat. Uneasy murmurs could be heard in the back and a few people slipped out the doors.

"I was saying," Brackenfeld stood, "that your son is not worthy of being chosen."

White lightening flooded the room once again, coming and going in all directions. Some of the sorcerers raised their wands others just sat and watched the light show.

"It would seem we are not alone," said Sanjay.

When the lightning stopped, Brackenfeld hissed, "You're doing this You've learned some exotic magic in your travels, and now you bring it here to scare us into letting you back on council. It's a boy's fireworks. Nothing more."

Sanjay shook his head. "My father sits on the council, and while he is alive, I have no need to sit with you. All I ask is to be one of the Brotherhood, one of the larger family."

"You want our knowledge and protection," said Grenchen.

"Yes, if you please," said Sanjay.

"But it seems to me, that you have greater power at your disposal than we can offer," said his father.

"I did not cause the lightning, nor do I understand why

it arrived. I have no control of it. This whole situation I've found myself in, is beyond my understanding."

Anton Wizenhall, the keeper of the histories, of the inner council spoke up. A short round man with rounded features, he wore thick glasses. "I must say, it is not without precedent. I remember reading stories about the elder council. There are not many, but they do exist. I had thought them myths, until now. I could do more research." He cleared his voice. "Whether we re-adopt Sanjay or not, we could at least give him our knowledge. Besides, if what Sanjay says is true, the fate of the whole world is at stake."

"Yes," said Grenchen, "I agree. I move we share our knowledge with Sanjay." Before debate could start, he continued. "And I call it to an immediate vote."

All the warlocks of the inner-circle stood except one. Brackenfeld. They tapped their staffs three times in favor of the motion.

"Passed. Sanjay you have our histories at your disposal. Wisenhall will help you with that."

"Thank you," Sanjay said. The pressure that had weighed so heavily on his chest lightened.

His father stood. "And I move that my son be fully reinstated to the Brotherhood."

"No," bellowed Brackenfeld. "That cannot be." He traced the scar on his cheek. "He attacked me, a member of the inner-council, and took my wife. He cannot be forgiven for this. He cannot be accepted as one of us. Ever."

Sanjay's hand tingled for his wand. Peregrine fluffed his wings.

"Does anyone else have something to say against my son?" asked Arjun Khan.

They shook their heads.

"I have something to say for your son," Grenchen said.

"I have heard rumors that Arianna, the wife Brackenfeld spoke of, was hospitalized for six months after she left him. She had been beaten and brutalized. Sanjay made sure she was taken care of and she now lives in hiding. We could call upon her to testify as to what actually happened that night and determine who was at fault."

Brackenfeld glared at the man.

Wisenhall stood. "The truth must come out. I move we start an investigation to end this feud for all time."

Murmurs flowed through the hall. Brackenfeld glared at everyone. Sanjay held his breath.

"Call to vote," declared Sanjay's father.

All but one of the inner-circle stood. They tapped their staffs three times.

"It is passed," declared Grimshaw, the chairman of the council. "Sanjay Khan's interference with Brackenfeld's family will be investigated. If it turns out he is innocent he will be re-instated. If it turns out he is guilty of abducting a woman against her will, then we will sentence him."

The staffs made of wood, as old as time, thumped three times.

SIXTEEN

"I need a coffee to go with my coffee."
~ Zoey Deschanel

Cassie woke up in the pre-dawn light feeling anxious. Every cell in her body twitched. She stretched her legs and wiggled her toes, but nothing relaxed her.

The morning broke beautifully into a perfect spring day. No signs of the storm from the day before remained. Sunshine bathed the land. In the distance, the snow-capped coastal mountains rose majestically from the deep blue sea. Cassie wished she could take a vacation from her life and enjoy Mystic Keep as if she were a tourist with no cares in this world.

But she couldn't.

Until Sanjay came to her with news about the portal, she figured her time was best spent looking for Larry's murderer. Gavin may be investigating the shooting, but he couldn't make people talk the way she could.

First on her to-do list was finding Ava, who hopefully would give her more leads. Second, she planned to see Kit again. Maybe he would remember something else about Larry that would help her investigation. Third, she would check out the leads Father Jacob gave her, the organist, and janitor. They had fallen to the bottom of her list as they just didn't sound evil enough.

CASSIE FOUND Ava in front of the city hall feeding the pigeons. Her shopping cart overflowed with garbage bags filled with stuff. Probably all her worldly possessions.

Ava smiled as she talked to the flock of birds that gathered around her. But her mouth dropped the moment Cassie approached.

"What do you want now?" she said.

"Good Morning, Ava. I'm not a Martian, by the way."

"I figured that, you damn fool. You speak English too good. No accent."

Cassie took a deep breath of the salty air. "I want to know more about Larry's life on the street, and I thought you could help me. I have more granola bars." She handed her a bag filled with food.

Ava squinted. "I told you what I know. It's the dark shadows. They probably did it." She leaned in and, in a conspiratorial tone, added, "They slink around town and steal people. I think they give the bodies to the Martians for food."

Food? Hmm. "The birds really like you," Cassie said.

"Yup, until my treats run out."

"Oh, well, I can do something about that. We always have scraps at The Perfect Brew. Just tell them I sent you and ask for a bag of stale bread."

The woman's hazel eyes reminded Cassie of the color of

the sky at dusk on a warm night. They brightened a smidge. "What's the catch?"

"No catch. But you could help me out by telling me more about Larry's life. You know, more about who he hung out with."

Ava took her hat off, looked up and squinted at the sun. Her dirty-blond hair fell to her shoulders. She scratched her head. "I don't know how much more I can tell you." She folded her arms and rocked herself.

Cassie nodded and looked at the pigeons. "I know Larry liked to bird watch. Did he ever have company?"

Ava screwed up her mouth. "Yeah. Sometimes. He spent hours in the park looking at birds. We have that in common." She licked her cracked lips. "Come to think of it. He started having company last month."

"Company?"

"Two men. I don't know their names. They're not from around here. They would come and sit with him for a bit."

"Can you describe them?"

"You know some people think because I live on the street, I'm stupid. But I'm not. I'm just poor, and when I don't have my meds, I go a little crazy. You give me ten dollars; I'll tell you anything you want to know."

Cassie handed the woman a ten-dollar bill.

"One was taller than you. The other shorter. Both wore dark clothes and sunglasses. The way they dressed and moved made me think of the FBI or the men in black, but I don't think they were good guys. Whenever they turned up, Larry shunned the rest of us and only talked to them. I think they were bad news."

Cassie nodded. "So, the tall guy. Did he look young or old?"

"Thirtyish, white, brown hair cut real short." She stuffed the bill in her pocket.

"Any distinguishing feature?"

Ava looked at the birds. "I never saw him up close. But, he had a bit of a limp."

"And the short guy?"

Ava rubbed her nose. "Short, stocky and bald. He acted like the sidekick. His skin was a cocoa color, but I couldn't tell if he was first nations, Hispanic, Polynesian, or south Asian. I can tell you he was super nervous. His head swiveled around like a damn owl. Gave me the creeps."

"Thanks, Ava. You've helped."

"Anything for Larry."

And, ten dollars Cassie smiled at her. "Did you tell the police any of this?"

"I don't talk to pigs."

Cassie grinned. She didn't want to resort to magic to see if Ava knew more. With Cassie's luck, she would turn her into a pigeon.

"Yeah, cops," Cassie said, "are a nuisance." She pushed her hair away from her face. "Catch you later, Ava. And don't forget you can always get a free coffee, and pigeon food at The Perfect Brew."

AS THEY WALKED over to the Bakery, Cassie asked Sid, "What do you think?"

"Pigeons taste stringy." Sid wiggled her whiskers.

"Seriously, that's all you got?"

"Ava is a straight-shooter. I believe her. She believes she sees shadows and aliens, but I'm guessing she's catching on to someone's magic. As to the two men ... they sound suspicious. That's all I got. You?"

"Same."

Kit was not in his usual slumber spot, so they continued their walk down the main street, and found him sitting outside the Barbershop playing chess.

Cassie decided to watch from a distance. After the chess match ended, he wandered up to the park and chatted with a group of four street people. One played the guitar. Then he rambled over to the city gym. Before he could disappear inside, she caught up with him.

"Hi Kit," she said.

"Hi, yourself. What's up?"

"I was wondering if you know *psycho guy*. Father Jacob said he punched Larry a few weeks ago."

"Oh yeah, everyone knows *the psycho*."

"Where can I find him?"

"You can't. He's dead."

"Dead?"

"Larry found him in the alley, last week, with a needle in his arm. Bad drugs."

"Bad, as in heroin?"

"Bad as in fentanyl."

"I'm sorry."

Kit shrugged. "He knew the risks." Kit looked up at the sun. "Look, I gotta go. The showers are only open for another half-hour."

MS. HERRINGBONE LIVED in a well-kept trailer on the outskirts of town, with flower boxes on every window. She answered her door in a fuzzy, pink housecoat and slippers. "I don't want any," she said and started sneezing into her elbow. Petite and square in shape, she had mousy brown hair pulled into a bun of some sort at the back of her head. Her gray eyes that looked hard enough to cut steel.

"I'm not selling any." Cassie said. "I'm a friend of Larry's ..."

The door half-closed. "You have a cat."

A panther actually, but she didn't say that. "Yes," Cassie said. "Her name is Sid. She's very well behaved."

"I hate cats."

Oh, please sweet goddess, don't say that, thought Cassie. But it was too late. Sid had slithered between the woman's feet into her house.

The organist screamed, turned, and chased him inside. Cassie followed the ruckus. The trailer was narrow, stuffy, and smelled like lavender. She followed the noise into the kitchen, which was bright yellow. On one wall hung a collection of tiny spoons; on the other, a crucifix. Sid sat on the counter with a sardine hanging out of her mouth.

"I'm so sorry," said Cassie giving the evil eye to her familiar. The woman shouldn't have said she didn't like cats. How could she get Sid out of the trailer?

"I'm allergic. And that's my lunch," Ms. Herringbone said, pointing to the fish.

Not anymore. "I'll just collect my cat and go."

"Get out of my house!" screamed the woman. "Out! Now! Out!"

Cassie frowned. "I will. I'm going." She hesitated on purpose. "As soon as you tell me about your relationship with Larry."

"Oh. If you must know," the woman snarled. "I didn't mind Larry." Her face had gone from angry-red to purple-rage. "But I didn't like him sleeping at the church. I don't believe the homeless belong in the church. It's a place for good Christians, after all. A place to worship."

The slurping sound of Sid digesting sardines was hard to ignore, but Cassie managed with a smile. "Do you own a gun?"

"Get out!" Ms. Herringbone screamed. "Or I'll call the police." She sneezed and grabbed a broom that leaned against the wall. With one wallop of a stroke, she swatted Sid off her counter.

The cat flew into the air and hissed as she turned and pounced on top of her.

Ms. Herringbone went down fast.

"I don't believe this," said a male voice behind her.

Oh, good goddess, no! I don't need an audience, thought Cassie. She turned.

Gavin stood filling the open doorway, looking all cop. "Ms. Black, what are you doing?"

"I just wanted to talk with the woman, and then Sid got away from me, and she chased her and ..."

"That woman is a menace," said the organist laying on the floor. Sid stood on her chest.

Sid snickered in Cassie's head. "Should I let her up?"

"You better let her up," said Cassie out loud for all to hear.

Gavin walked over and helped the older woman to her feet. "Don't worry, I'll see Ms. Black out."

With his hand at the small of Cassie's back, he ushered her out the front door and closed it behind them. Sid followed with her tail held high.

Should Cassie spell him, or just play dumb? Before she made up her mind, he spoke.

"That was stupid. Ms. Herringbone carries a panic button in her pocket. She hit it as soon as she saw you."

"I didn't mean to scare her. I just wanted to know ..."

"More about Larry. I know, Ms. Black."

It was never a good sign when he called her that.

"You're trying to find out who shot Larry."

She nodded.

"The organist doesn't own a gun. She's never shot a gun. She's not violent. No detective would put her on a suspect list."

"She got violent with me," said Sid in Cassie's head.

Cassie laughed.

Gavin's denim blue eyes narrowed. "What's so funny."

"You said she's not violent, but she took a broom to Sid."

A smirk cracked his hardass cop-face. "I would have liked to have seen that."

"Do you have time to come for coffee?" she asked. He must have information to share by now.

"No," he said. "Sorry. I'm in the middle of a murder investigation. Just do me a favor, Ms. Black, and don't get in my way."

"I THINK you should get in his way," said Sid in Cassie's head as they walked away. "I can think of many ways you can do that.' Her tail stood straight up, and she stalked into the sunlit afternoon, as only a feline high on sardines and snark could.

Cassie didn't bother answering her. It would only encourage her familiar's overactive libido. Besides, the mysterious two men in sunglasses nagged at Cassie. She headed to The Brew to see if anyone there knew anything about them.

She could smell rain. Dark clouds gathered above, and a chill dampened the air. Another storm was moving in, and in the distance, a dog barked.

SEVENTEEN

"Coffee is vital for survival. Dinosaurs didn't have coffee and look how tht turned out." ~ FB

When Cassie and Sid returned to The Brew, they found it filled to capacity. They took a seat at their favorite table by the fireplace and watched everyone coming and going for a while. A perfect brew arrived in front of Cassie three seconds after she plopped down in the chair. She looked up to see who had spelled her drink. Brianna smiled back. Cassie mouthed thank you and settled in for her first sip.

There was a comfortable mix of supernatural and ordinary beings in the milieu. No arguing wizards today, thank the goddess. Joni Mitchell sang over the speakers, and Cassie soaked in the comforting vibes.

When the coffee line thinned, she approached the bar where the two head baristas stood. Oscar and Brianna had been with The Brew from its first day. Skilled kitchen witches, they were hexing the espresso machine.

"I gotta question for you," Cassie said to them.

Oscar looked up. "Shoot."

"I heard that Larry was talking to two strangers in town. According to Ava, they looked like two men in black. You know dark clothes, sunglasses, and serious expressions. The taller one, a Caucasian, had a limp, and the other was dark-skinned, short, stocky, and bald. Does that description ring any bells?"

As she looked into Oscar's artic-blue eyes, she lost herself for a moment. It was no wonder the women called him Thor behind his back. He stood over six feet, and his Nordic good looks were simply intoxicating. He scrunched up his face. "They haven't come in here, on my shifts."

Brianna worked mornings. Cassie turned to her, hoping that maybe she would know something. In her late twenties, the barista had the figure of a runway model, auburn hair, and sage-green eyes. She nodded as she heard the description of the men. "Nope. I don't think I've seen them, either. You know Ava sees aliens. Right?"

Cassie laughed. "Yeah, I heard all about them. Thanks anyway."

"I'll let you know if I see them," said Oscar.

Cassie and Sid headed up to her apartment. When they got there, Sid meowed.

"What now?" asked Cassie.

"I know that look on your face. You've got a plan."

"Maybe. Why shouldn't I have a plan?"

"I need tuna first."

"I can't believe you're still hungry." Cassie fed her and sat down at the kitchen table with a piece of paper and a pen. "I'm going to make a suspect list." She drew columns and made headings on top of them: Name, Motive, Means, Opportunity, Alibi, Other. "I can't think of anything else."

"Magic. You've left out magic."

Cassie added a seventh column, titled Magic.

"I won't list Ms. Herringbone or Psycho Guy as we've ruled them out."

Under the Name category, she wrote: Limper, Baldy, Father Jacob, and Kit. She read over the names and added X.

"Who's x?" asked Sid.

"Someone I can't identify yet."

Sid's whiskers twitched. "As in something that slithered out of the portal? As in Ophelia's murderer? As in your poisoner?"

"Yeah, that's what I was thinking."

The cat licked her paw. "It's a start, Sherlock."

The sound of an incoming text rang on Cassie's cell phone. She looked at it. "Sanjay's invited us up to his place for dinner in an hour."

"Us?"

Cassie checked out her guest room. Where was Jane? "I'll send her a text to come home, and we'll go up together."

Sid chuckled in her panther way.

"What? Don't you think Sanjay can cook?"

"It's not that. I'm sure our rogue warlock can access simple culinary magic."

"What then?"

"I wonder if he knows what he's doing, having two Black witches for guests?"

She laughed. Sid had a point. Whenever a part of the Black clan gathered, stuff happened. Meals were never a regular event for them. "Hopefully, he'll have some news from the Brotherhood." Cassie ran a hand through her tousled hair. "Listen, I'm going to take a nap." Sid beat her to the bed, and they both fell into a deep sleep.

Thirty minutes later, Jane arrived with coffees in hand

to find Cassie drenched in sweat and twisting and turning on the mattress. Jane nudged her.

Sid woke instantly. "What happened?"

Jane shook her sister. "Cassie. Cassie. Wake up." But her eyes didn't open. "Sid, get the warlock. Fast." As the familiar disappeared, Jane snapped her fingers to run a cold bath and snapped them again to deliver Cassie's trembling body into it. Cassie groaned as her body slid beneath the cold water, and her body shook, but her eyes did not open.

SID, in her full panther form, crashed through Sanjay's front door. Sanjay didn't ask what was wrong, he knew by a feeling deep in his bones, Cassie was in trouble. With a flick of his wrist, he created a portal and returned with Sid to Cassie's apartment. Jane stood over her sister, invoking a healing spell, but it wasn't working.

Knowing their combined power would be stronger than one of them alone, he grabbed her hand and started a warlock chant of his own.

They chanted over and over again until the air turned icy cold, and blue mist surrounded them. Cassie opened her eyes.

With magic, they pulled her out of the tub. On the bathroom floor, she vomited until nothing remained in her system. Jane used her magic to dress Cassie in a fresh nightgown. Sanjay picked her up in his arms and carried her to her bed.

IT TORE SANJAY APART, seeing Cassie so weak and vulnerable. As he stroked her forehead with magic, he gritted his jaw. "Blessed be the power of light," he chanted.

As he ran his fingers over her temple, Cassie mumbled. He turned to Jane. "What did she eat?"

Sid, who had returned to her scruffy house cat form, answered. "The last thing she had was a coffee downstairs prepared by Brianna." Her feline eyes burned with anger. "Go, warlock. I will protect her."

"Go," repeated Jane. "I will stay with her, as well."

Sanjay transported himself downstairs, to stand behind the coffee bar inches from Oscar.

Oscar took a step back from the warlock who vibrated with anger.

"Where is Brianna," Sanjay asked.

Oscar looked around. "She was here a minute ago." He looked again. "What's happened?"

"She poisoned Cassie."

Oscar dropped the cup he held in his hand. It crashed to the tile floor, sending a magic potion splashing over their feet. "Brianna? I never would have thought. Brianna? How?"

Sanjay exhaled noisily. "Where would she go?"

A FEW FEET AWAY, Detective Gavin MacGregor sat with another cop. How the hell did Sanjay just appear like that? And what's this about poison? He stood up. "Sanjay, did you say Cassie's been poisoned? Again?"

AS SANJAY'S hands rose in the air, he pulled magic from every cell of his body and pushed it outwards, swirling a spell over the room, "I call on the powers that be, hear my plea. So, the guilty may be found, I must look around. Freeze the mundanes." He paused. "So, mote it be." A light mist rose from the floor and swirled around the room. The norms froze, and the supernaturals looked to Sanjay.

"We must find Brianna. I believe she poisoned Cassie, and possibly Ophelia." He held his spell steady. "Or, she knows who did. Who can help me?"

A wolf shifter in the back stood up. "I saw her mount her Harley out back, five minutes ago. She headed north on the main road."

Donavan O'Reilly, the warlock, stood up. A tall, slender man of Irish descent, he had black hair that fell straight to his shoulders and crystal blue eyes. A light scruff covered his masculine face. He wore a black warlock cape. "I will form a posse and find her."

Sanjay nodded. "So be it."

O'Reilly's cape flew up, and he disappeared, along with several others in the room.

EIGHTEEN

"Espresso is to Italy what wine is to France."
~ Charles Maurice de Talleyrand

Cassie tossed and turned in her unconscious state. A dark figure chased her through a maze, and she couldn't find a way out. Every turn she took led to a dead end. Overhead, demonized crows swooped and dived at her head. Holding her arms above her for protection, she ducked and weaved. Holding her breath, she took the next turn. Dead end. And the next corner. Dead end. Raising her eyes to the sky, she screamed a silent scream.

All the while, the figure drew closer. Closer and closer. Cassie didn't need to look back to see him. She could feel him. As he drew nearer, his essence crept into her bones, and like a poison worked its way through her body. "Do not fight me, Cassiopeia," it whispered.

"No," she screamed, but again, no sound left her mouth. She took a deep breath and increased her speed, trying not to stumble over the tangle of roots that now impeded her pathway. If she fell, even once, he would be on her.

"There is no point in running, my dear. Sooner or later, you will be mine."

Not if I have anything to do with it, she thought.

He chuckled like a mad-man.

Faster and faster, she ran chasing down every path she found, but no exit came into view. There was no escape. She was trapped.

The dark figure would have her.

He chuckled again.

Creep! Should she stop and wait for him to catch up? Maybe she could kick him in his most precious bits or scratch his eyes out. Who was she fooling? He would be strong and unbeatable. Such was the nature of darkness. A sudden overwhelming desire to just give up paralyzed her mind. She stopped and waited.

The dark figure slowed his pace as he approached her. Ten-feet tall, and more demon than human, he stood before her. He wore a black cloak with a hood that obscured his face. She would have thought this would be the most terrifying moment of her life, but it wasn't. The desire to be a part of him, a part of something stronger than herself, grew in her heart. What had he done to her?

He smiled an evil grin. "Gottcha."

Thunder rumbled, lightning ripped through the sky, and the ground trembled. The air smelt sweeter, like her sister's perfume. Maybe it was a dream, but she thought she saw Peregrine flying high above. Were they rescuing her?

"CASSIE, LISTEN TO ME," demanded Sanjay. "We are here on the other side, waiting for you. No matter what you see, it is not the truth. Ignore it. Tell your mind, tell your heart, to fight it. And reach out for us."

"Cassie, come to us," echoed Jane.

Was this all a dream? Cassie took one more look at the dark figure, imprinting him in her memory.

He chuckled. "I will be back for you."

"Who are you?"

"I am Erebus, born of Chaos. I have been cast to live in the shadows since the dawn of time. Now, I have come to earth through your portal. I will rise and take my rightful place in this world. I, the Lord of Darkness, will reign."

Cassie's heart pounded in her throat. Her mind ached with confusion.

"Cassie," she could hear her friends calling for her. "Cassie, come back to us."

Grabbing her crystal talisman tightly in her hand, she squeezed her eyes shut. "Blessed be the power of light. Blessed be the power of light. Blessed be the power of light. For I am a child of the light."

A flash of bright, white light rocked through her mind, and the power of the darkness left her body. Opening her eyes, she found herself in her apartment. Jane and Sanjay stood over her, with worried expressions on their faces.

Together they chanted, "Blessed be the power of light."

All sensations returned to her at once, with the force of a sledgehammer. She rubbed her forehead. "What happened?"

"You are safe, and that's all that matters," said Sanjay, who grabbed her hand and held it firmly in his. "I'll give you some privacy. But I won't be far. I'll wait in the other room." He squeezed her hand and vanished.

"Is he always so formal?" asked Jane. "He's obviously in love with you."

Cassie didn't know what to say. Relief poured through every single cell in her body. "Jane, I almost gave in."

Her sister helped her sit up. "But you didn't. That's all that matters now." I'll wait with the warlock.

Cassie watched her sister vanish and wondered. It would have been so easy to give in, and for a moment, she truly wanted to. What did that say about her? What did that say about the safety of the realm?

TIME SLOWED as Sanjay waited for Cassie to appear. The depth of his feelings hit him like a ton of steel cauldrons. In his weaker moments, he had acknowledged to himself that she was pretty and funny, and, well, different than any other witch he had ever met. But he had no idea of his true feelings until this happened. He knew he should be worried about the portal door and the safety of the earth, but all he could think about was her. He could not—would not—lose her. 'Mine,' said a voice deep within him Mine.

Jane joined him on the sofa and patted his shoulder. "Cassie grows on you, kind of like mold. You'll get used to it," she said.

Grows? Is that what happened. He had never fallen for a woman like this before. Maybe, falling in true love was similar to a fatal disease. His chest tightened.

Cassie appeared in jeans and a blue sweatshirt, with her hair styled and her make-up witch perfect. But, Sanjay noted, the color of her skin was off, and her heartbeat slower than usual. He waved his hand. Sparks flew through the air, and a setting for high-tea appeared on the coffee table. Complete with scones that smelled like heaven, jams, and petit fours, it looked like something out of Good-Witch blog. A steaming pot of tea and cups stood beside it.

"Wow," said Jane. "I'm impressed."

"Have something to eat," Sanjay said to Cassie. "You'll feel better."

Jane poured tea, and they each chose goodies to nibble on. It was the sort of domestic sight you might see anywhere in the world, he thought. Sanjay had made tea for his family! What kind of rogue warlock was he becoming?

CASSIE DOWNED THREE SANDWICHES, one with an egg salad filling, one with cream cheese and cucumber, and one with smoked salmon. Delicious. She drank two cups of tea and wondered, not for the first time, why any thirsty person would bother with such a small cup. "Who knew fighting evil would make you feel so hungry?" she said.

Jane smiled at Cassie. Sanjay looked uncomfortable as if his shirt was two sizes too small. She wondered what was going on in his mind. Sid pawed and drooled on her feet.

"It was awful," she said. "The beast's name is Erebus."

Sanjay dropped his cup, and he whipped his other hand into the air to use magic to put the tea back into it and place it on the table. "The Lord of Darkness."

"Yes," said Cassie. "We are fighting, The Erebus."

NINETEEN

"They say dark matter holds the universe together. The only dark matter my universe needs is coffee." ~ Cassie

Would this day ever end, thought Cassie as she curled into a fetal position under two layers of quilts. They spent hours discussing the history of Erebus and what they could do to fight him, The Primordial Evil Deity. Until this day, they had thought Erebus was a mythical being.

What could they possibly do against such power? Erebus was the origin of all darkness. He wasn't just a big, bad mean guy. He was the biggest, baddest, mean guy—evil personified. Cassie bit her bottom lip.

The warmth of Sid's body against hers gave her comfort. Jane went to bed first and retired to the guest room. Sanjay wouldn't leave no matter how many hints she gave him, so Cassie gave him a sheet and blankets for the couch.

Cassie appreciated him wanting to protect her, but the truth was that if Erebus wanted her, he would find her.

Tomorrow when she felt stronger, she would talk with the rest of her family. Maybe someone would know someone who knew something. In her hand, the crystal amulet her father had given her for her sixteenth birthday cut into her skin. Her limbs trembled, and her head ached. Determined to get some sleep, she played the ambient sounds of a waterfall and worked on deep breathing. But sleep evaded her, and the cold air in the room embraced her.

Wait. It shouldn't be cold in this room. The day had been warm. Sitting straight up in bed, she snapped on the overhead light. At the end of her bed, stood Alessandro.

Mixed feelings of elation and horror tore through her mind. Not now. Just not now, she thought.

"I felt your fear, my love." His voice was low and guttural, quintessential vampire.

Sid's ears went back. "The vampire is back."

Cassie took him in. Seven feet of sweet, Italian, male paradise with fangs. He wore ripped, blue jeans and a white dress shirt over a six-pack that had been hard for over a century. His long mahogany-brown hair had been pulled back into a ponytail, revealing high cheekbones and choco-late-brown eyes that she could swim in. He was more hand-some than any man ought to be. More dangerous than any vampire ought to be. But he was hers, in a way. Her vampire. She had lived with him for five years, and while he had talked of forever, she had enjoyed the moment.

He sniffed the air. "You are not alone, my love."

Sanjay appeared at the side of her bed. His wand in his right hand vibrated with power. "Is this your vampire connection?" he asked. His eyes fixed on Alessandro with a deathly stare as he pulled up a wall of fire between them.

Cassie waved at Sanjay. "Put your wand away. He won't hurt us."

A wicked smile played on Alessandro's lips. "I don't know about that. I think it might be fun to hurt *him*."

The energy between the men felt combustible as if just one wrong word would send them flying at each other, like a match to dynamite.

"Sanjay, this is Alessandro, the man I was living within Amsterdam. Alessandro, this is Sanjay Kahn, a friend."

"Oh, goody. A man-witch to bleed," Alessandro said. "I haven't fed on a warlock for many a year."

The bedroom door banged open. "Interesting company," Jane announced as she entered the room. "Are they fighting over you?"

"No," the men said in unison.

Cassie rubbed the spot between her eyes, where her head hurt the most. "I'm not up to a stand-off. Jane transport us out of here.'

"No," repeated the men, again in unison. They looked at each other with derision.

Alessandro folded his arms. "I am here because I felt Cassie's fear. Is she in danger?"

"I protect her," said Sanjay.

"She is not yours to protect, warlock," said the vampire.

"Oh, this just keeps getting better," said Jane, who pulled her cell phone out to video the event. "All I need is popcorn." Sid jumped up on her shoulder.

"Put that away, little sister," said Alessandro. "I see she sleeps alone, so the warlock is not her chosen man."

"I protect her with my life," said Sanjay.

The vampire nodded. "Let us talk about the danger she is in."

"So mature," remarked Jane to Cassie. "Don't you just want to stir the cauldron a bit? Maybe show your nightgown off, or something."

Alessandro's fangs descended, and he snarled at Jane.

She put a hand over her mouth. "Okay then, I'll be quiet." Sid snickered.

The vampire turned to the warlock. "When you live as long as I have, you learn to ignore your lover's occasional need for others. I will talk in private with Cassie about that matter later. Right now, I want to know who hunts her."

"Erebus," said Cassie, who didn't want to say his name out loud, for fear it would give him some power. But, she wanted to get this conversation over with as fast as she could, with the least amount of magic and fang. "The Erebus."

Alessandro's dark eyes drew together. "Why would he chase you?"

SANJAY LOWERED HIS WAND, and the wall of fire disappeared. He hated vampires. They were even more arrogant than warlocks. But this man had power, and he cared for Cassie. Perhaps he could help them.

He sniffed the air. Vampires smelled like blood and death, and it turned his stomach. Alessandro may say he loves Cassie, but Sanjay doubted a species as violent as bloodsuckers were capable of love. She was his to protect.

As Cassie explained how she had inherited the portal and the curse that went with it, Sanjay watched the vampire. He was built like a freaking tank. There had to be some spell to take him down. Why had Cassie lived with *him*? Were vampires that great in bed?

ALESSANDRO TURNED TO THE WARLOCK. "I offer my assistance. I am not a guardian of the portal, but I will help defend it for Cassie's sake. I have friends who will help as well."

"Yoo-hoo, we're still here," said Jane with a voice dripping with youthful sarcasm.

Alessandro snarled and gave her a menacing sideglance, and his fangs glistened once more.

Cassie was just about to suggest they gathered in the living room when a knock came on her front door. They looked at each other.

"Police open up." The voice was loud and clear.

"What the hell!" said Alessandro.

"Oh, the local cop has a thing for Cassie," said Jane. "She forgot to add that. He probably thinks he's saving her from something big and mean." Her brows danced with mischief.

Alessandro's eyes crossed. "What do they put in the water around here?"

Cassie stood. "Calm down. Gavin suspects I'm a witch, and he doesn't want magic in his town. Let's not get him more suspicious."

The pounding continued.

"You're not telling lover-vamp the whole story," said Sanjay with a self-satisfied smirk. "You kissed him."

Cassie rounded on the warlock. "How? How the hex did you know?"

The voice from below got louder. Gavin must have been using a megaphone. "If you don't open up, we'll have to ..."

Sanjay teleported the witches to the door. "Answer it," he said to Cassie.

"You spied on me," she said to Sanjay. The thought of him watching her kiss Gavin made her cheeks burn.

"Just answer the stupid door."

Jane giggled. "This is more fun than watching a movie." She conjured up a bag of popcorn dripping with butter.

Cassie opened up the door to find Gavin and Extra-Hot staring at them. "Hi, Gavin. Is something wrong? It's got to be at least midnight."

Gavin's face dropped. "I thought." He paused and looked at the ground. "I thought something had happened to you."

"As you can see, I'm fine."

GAVIN WALKED FORWARD into the room, eyeing Sanjay, who looked agitated, Jane with her popcorn, and Cassie. "Earlier today, I heard something about poisoning." He looked past them and saw a stranger standing by the fire with his arms crossed. He did a doubletake. The freaking man was huge. Gavin's right hand found the top of his holster. Too big to be normal. They all must be hostages.

"As I said, Gavin, I'm fine," Cassie lied in as reassuring a voice as she could muster.

Gavin came closer to her. "Are you sure?"

"A hundred percent."

"I haven't met *him*," Gavin said, pointing at Alessandro.

And you don't want to, thought Cassie. "Oh, that's a friend from out of town."

"Has he got a name?"

Alessandro walked forward with his predatory stride. "I'm Alessandro from Amsterdam."

"Oh," said Gavin. Extra-Hot looked at the floor as if fascinated by the vampire's sized fifteen running shoes.

Cassie prayed to the universe that Alessandro wouldn't eat the friendly cops. While the vampire played nice with most of her friends, he did have a nasty history of eliminating policemen when they got in his way. She cleared her throat. "Detective, this is a private party."

His denim blue eyes locked with hers. "You're drawing a lot of strange men, Ms. Black."

Jane laughed. Sid purred.

"That she is," said Sanjay, stepping forward. "Rest assured that Cassie Black is well-spoken for." He didn't need to use magic. Gavin took one look at his eyes and left.

As the door closed, Sanjay turned and faced Cassie.

She opened her mouth, but before she could speak, the warlock said, "Deal with it."

TWENTY

"Wake up and smell the coffee." ~Ann Landers

Cassie woke up in the morning to a home full of visitors. Jane lay on her right snoring, while Sid slept on her left twitching. Sanjay, who had reappeared in the middle of the night, slept in a reclining chair outside her bedroom door. With his hair mussed up and muscles relaxed, he looked even more handsome than usual, kind of vulnerable and less controlling. Alessandro lay in a coffin, Sanjay conjured for him in the guest room closet. It appeared they had accepted one another's presence. Still, it would take only one mishap, and they would be at each other's throats. Two magic men in one house were two too many.

Thankfully Gavin had left the night before right after their short conversation. Did Sanjay use a sophisticated spell to fix things? Maybe. When the three men shot daggers from their eyes at each other, his fingers had danced at his side. The distinct smell of ripe peaches lingered. With his usual detached coolness, Alessandro simply sneered at him and folded his arms.

When the door closed behind the cop, Alessandro said. "We need a plan."

Men and plans! Goddess help her. She went to bed twenty minutes later, before they could create a checklist or an app that detailed her bathroom schedule.

Jane stirred and moaned. "Tell me, it's not morning."

"It's morning, sunshine." Somehow that never grew old.

Sid meowed. "Not so loud. Yesterday was long and wicked."

"You're telling me this?" answered Cassie. She threw the covers off the three of them. "I'm going downstairs for coffee."

Jane grabbed the blankets and pulled them over herself. "I need more sleep. If a shadow gets you, it's not on me."

Sid sniffed the air. "They're both still here."

"Of course, they are." Cassie clothed herself in ripped jeans and a long black tunic. Rubbing her hands together, she mumbled a transportation spell to land herself in the coffee shop. Never had she garnered so much male attention, and though she might have fantasized about having three hot men interested in her at the same time, it wasn't fun. It was suffocating. They all had plans for her. She needed to get past Sanjay and escape.

"Oh, no," grumbled Sid, whose ears pulled back and whiskers quivered. "You're not going to spell us."

"Unus, duo, tres." She snapped her fingers, and they wooshed into the stratosphere and landed back in the main biffy. Darn it all. What she would give to have her magic work for a change.

Sanjay opened the door to find her sitting on the throne. "What are you doing?" His voice croaked from lack of sleep.

"Do you mind. I'd like some privacy," Cassie said.

"Cassie, you need to tell us where you're going."

"You set wards to keep me in the apartment, didn't you?"

He ran a hand over his face. "I may have."

Through clenched teeth, she muttered. "I just wanted to go downstairs for coffee."

SANJAY EXHALED NOISILY and crossed his arms. He needed to think, but his mind hadn't woke up yet. Hot damn! She looked beautiful. Her skin radiated wholesome goodness. He laughed at himself. Never had he chased that before in his life, and now it called to him. 'Mine,' said his inner voice. "Cassie, you need to be reasonable," he said out loud.

Cassie stood and glared at him. She stepped closer. "You have no right to hold me prisoner, warlock. Wait. Just wait ..."

"Until what? Until you tell your daddy? I'm sure he would agree with me that you need protection. Wait until you tell your vampire? The big, bad bloodsucker is dead to the world, sleeping soundly in a coffin I conjured for him. Besides which, do you really think he would dare suck my royal, warlock blood? I'm not an easy kill, and if he succeeded, he would ignite an unholy vampire-warlock war such as the world has never seen." Sanjay traced her cheek with his fingers. Her skin felt so soft.

"And," he said, "killing me would not bring you any closer to his dead heart. I remind you, he has a dead heart, as in dead and gone, long gone. He's had enough women to fill a football field. You're just another ..." He stopped.

Her soft lips trembled. Urgh! He felt like a cad. Did anyone use that word anymore? They should. It so fit. He cleared his throat. "Cassie, we have to talk about ..."

Her brows rose. "What? What do we have to talk about now? We're in the biffy. Don't tell me. Another app?"

Anger made her cheeks redden in the most delicious way, and her breasts rose, which caused a part of him to rise. "Later then." he said. "We need to talk later. About us." He snapped his fingers.

CASSIE FELT SO angry at him she could bite, but other feelings swirled inside her as well. Feelings that had grown too strong to ignore. Us! He said Us!

Not now. I can't deal with 'us' now, she thought. She wandered over to her favorite table, by the fireplace, and plunked herself down. She put her head in her hands.

Sid appeared on the chair opposite her, a gift, no doubt, from the warlock. "Cassie," she said.

"Shush." Familiars could be altogether too familiar This wasn't the time.

"Cassie?"

"No. Just no."

"Cassie, listen..."

"No, no, and no. You're going to tell me to play dirty with the boys. That's just too much to think about right now."

A second later. "Cassie."

"What?" Of all the cat familiars in the world, why did she get the most persistent?

Sid raised her head, and her tail thumped on the cushion. "I have one thing to say to you. Listen to your heart."

Huh?

Sid laid down and stretched out for a nap.

Cats!

The smell of coffee and magic revived Cassie, as a

steaming cup of brew materialized in front of her. She looked over at Oscar, who stood behind the coffee bar and nodded. He smiled back.

Her magic brew hit her in all the right places, and her mind began to clear. With help, she had won her battle with Erebus.

Alessandro and Sanjay would use their contacts to find out more about the beast and how he could be defeated. Jane would access the witch's community, and Donovan O'Reilly had a posse looking for Brianna. Her friends had united to protect her and the world. A deep sense of gratitude swelled in her heart.

It was time to sit back and let things unfold. They would find a solution. Cassie bit her lip. She had never been one to sit around. She could search for Larry's murderer.

"Are you crazy?" asked Sid, who opened one eye.

"Seriously? Can we not get through one day without you questioning my sanity?" replied Cassie.

"Erebus is not just a boogeyman, he's THE boogeyman, and he's after *you*. You need to lay low, lady. Leave the human murder to Gavin. He's a trained detective."

"Hmm." Cassie tossed her hair away from her face. "I'm sure Gavin is good at police paperwork, but you and I both know he can't question people the way I can."

Sid's whiskers twitched. "Good grief."

TWENTY MINUTES and a successful escape spell later, they walked along the street looking for clues. When Oscar figured out she had left the building, he would tell Sanjay, so she had to work fast.

Spring sunshine glistened over the landscape, making

everything seem new and shiny. The calm after the storm. The smell of cherry blossoms perfumed the gentle breeze that caressed her face. In the distance, an eagle called to his mate.

"I'm going back to the priest," said Cassie as they rounded the corner.

"Why the priest?" asked Sid.

"Just a hunch. Father Jacob knows something he's not telling us."

FATHER JACOB GAVE her a paternal smile as she walked up the aisle towards him. Her witch senses twitched. Something was off. Could she trust her insights in a place like this? This should be the safest place in town, a place where people came to worship the divine. Sacred ground.

Jacob Greepsly's smile broke his otherwise somber face.

"Hi," she said, "Where were you the night Larry died?"

"Well, good morning to you, too." He chuckled and looked towards the figure of Christ on the cross. "I spent the night in my bungalow, behind the church."

"Alone?"

"Yes."

"No, alibi?"

His heartbeat quickened. The smell of sweat sliding down his back, stung Cassie's nostrils. He had more to tell.

"No, Ms. Black. I have no one to corroborate my whereabouts on the night of Larry's death. I'm surprised you ask. Surely, you don't suspect me?"

Before he started sweating, she hadn't. She had only hoped her question would stir the cauldron enough to get him to tell her more. Now she wondered. "How long did you know Larry?"

"Ms. Black, I haven't time for your silliness."

Silliness? Cassie straightened her back and silently spelled him to say more.

The priest blinked. "I will not talk." He shook. "I cannot talk." The color of his face turned red. "They would kill me." He blinked and blinked and blinked, as he fought her magic.

She never trusted things that happened in threes. It took all her energy to hold her magic in place. "Who would kill you?"

The church door opened wide, and the children's choir spilled inside. Twelve pre-adolescent kids laughing and joking ran up the aisle. Cassie released her spell on the cleric.

He exhaled noisily. "Thank you," he whispered, and he turned his attention to the children as if nothing had happened.

But it had. "I'll be back," said Cassie.

NEXT ON HER list was Kit. This time she found him in his usual doorway behind the Bakery smoking a cigarette. In the early morning sun, the alley looked like a party gone wrong. The smell of vomit rose above other putrid smells. Rats feasted on scraps. Crows circled above. How could anyone hang out here?

Since her direct approach had worked on the priest, she decided to use it again. "Good morning, Kit. Where were you the night Larry died?"

Kit looked at her with blurry eyes. "A gentleman doesn't tell."

"Oh." Cassie hadn't expected that answer. "Not even when there's a murder?"

His mouth twitched. "I may be homeless, but that doesn't mean you can pin the murder on me. For your information, I'm not the murdering kind of man."

"Tell me her name." And please don't tell me you did the nasty in this alley. That was one image Cassie could do without. She spelled him to spill his secrets.

"Melinda Goodtimes. She's a barmaid and has a room above the Rusty Anchor." That was the main watering hole for the mundane in town. "We hook up now and then. That night I was with her."

"Thank you," said Cassie. She would check on that story later. "Do you know anything about two suspicious-looking men coming and going in town."

Kit smirked. "There are more than two strange men around here. Did you see that tall Italian who arrived last night?"

Cassie winced. "I may have."

"Huh. So, the pale giant's a friend of yours?"

"Yeah, and he's okay." She crossed her fingers behind her back as she lied. "Ava said she saw two strange men. I was wondering about them."

Kit took a long draw on his cigarette. "Drug dealers," he said. He exhaled smoke rings in the air.

"Drugs?" That shouldn't surprise her. It was a port town after all. But still, it was her port town, and the thought of drugs made her shiver.

"Yeah, they bring in opioids, heroin, fentanyl whatever people ask for, and take out money."

Cassie groaned. She could never cut it as a cop. Who wanted to know about the seedy underbelly of their community? Not her.

Sid's cold nose brushed her leg. "Remember, it's for Larry," she said in her mind.

Cassie looked up to the sky. "Who is their connection in town."

Kit looked at her with hooded eyes. "Not sure. Not sure I want to know, either. I don't get involved."

"Do you know where they hang out? If you do, you gotta tell me. For Larry."

He looked down at the ground and shuffled his feet. "The church."

"Thanks," she said. Acting on a hunch that Kit knew more than he was saying, she asked, "Anything else you can tell me about Larry's life that might help me find his murderer?"

Kit drew hard on his cigarette butt and exhaled. "Nah."

A gray-striped tomcat pounced on a rat a few feet from them, and a fight ensued. Loud meows and crunching sounds filled Cassie's ears. Talk about a sign to move on!

"That's life for ya," said Kit. "It's always a battle for survival."

Cassie looked at him. "So, you got nothing else?"

Peregrine landed on a trash bin and stared at her. When she ignored him, he made clicking sounds.

Cassie exhaled loudly. "I wish we knew Larry's last name.

Kit leaned back. "As far as I'm concerned, a man's past is his past. If he doesn't want to share it, that's his business. Larry didn't want us to know his last name. End of story."

"But surely there's someone out there who cares about him."

Kit stared at something behind her. She turned. There stood Gavin MacGregor looking almost as angry as he did when she hit his sportscar. Almost.

"What are you doing?" he asked Cassie.

"I'm checking out the garbage in town," she lied. "Kit was telling me the areas he thinks need cleaning the most."

"Uh-huh." His cop face said he didn't believe a word.

"I'm out of here." Kit said as he walked away.

"Ms. Black," said Gavin with a scowl.

"Ms. Black? Really, Gavin. What's with the Ms? Do I need to remind you we've kissed?"

His face turned scarlet. "Do I need to remind you that it's my job to chase the bad guys?"

"If it makes you feel better, sure," she said. "But, I'm the one who should be offended."

"And why is that?" Gavin squinted.

"You barged into my home last night and disturbed my guests."

A smile slid across his handsome face. "Tough for you."

"You had no right," she said.

"I thought you were in danger. And who is that big man? The pale guy."

"My former boyfriend."

"Oh."

"Any more questions?"

Gavin firmed his jaw. "Cassie, I'm not sure what you're up to, but I'm worried about you. I don't like the company you keep." He cleared his throat. "Let me be straight with you. I think you're in danger. I can feel it. I want you to know that I would move heaven and earth to protect you and my town."

Nice. "Thanks, Gavin."

"Mmm. Even if it turns out you are a witch, I will protect you. It's my job. But I can't help you if you don't let me know what's going on."

Hah! Where should she begin? Witch? There were

many things she could say. But instead, she turned and stomped off. Let Gavin figure things out for himself. She needed to deal with a warlock.

Peregrine made a hoarse screech and took flight.

TWENTY-ONE

"Coffee is language itself."
~ Jackie Chan

In her apartment Cassie found Jane drawing on a sketch pad at the kitchen table. The smell of home-brewed coffee and freshly baked scones filled the room. Cassie sat and teleported for herself a cup of coffee and a scone, and a bowl of milk and a scone for Sid. Her magic was definitely improving. Could it be a side-effect of the poison? There's a random thought.

Cassie took a sip of her drink, hot, full-bodied, and creamy, the coffee was just the way she liked it. "What are you drawing?" she asked Jane.

Jane turned her pad so Cassie could see her sketch. With lines and shading, her sister had drawn a picture of a white van with a large logo on the side, which read: '1-800-Got-Witch.'

Cassie's stomach plummeted. "You've got to be kidding." So much for keeping a low profile in Dodge.

"I had a vision."

Lordy! Lordy! Jane and her visions.

Her sister shrugged. "I saw myself, Cassie. I was happier than I have ever been. I drove a white van that rode on magic, not gas. Cool, eh. No emissions." Then she giggled. "I went to people's houses and helped them. I gave an old lady a potion to stop her hair from falling out, an old man a virility boost, and a teenager an anti-anxiety potion. White magic. Nothing but white magic." Her eyes gleamed. "The dream turned into a giant jigsaw puzzle that fell apart piece by piece and landed in my heart. That's how I know it was a true vision." Her face glowed. "You know, Cassie if I dream it ..."

"You do it. Yeah, I know." And things worked out, usually, until they didn't. "Remember Charlie, your so-called steady boyfriend in sixth grade who kissed your best friend at a party?"

"Yeah, I remember. I gave him smelly farts for a week, and no one would talk to him. He had got what was coming to him."

"Maybe, but you couldn't call that white magic. It fell in the gray zone, and as a result, Mom gave you weeding duty for a month."

"Okay. I won't cast farts. What's your point?"

Cassie exhaled slowly. One thing she had learned from having five sisters, was the importance of being direct but tactful. "I'm worried that you may think you're doing the right thing, but it may not be. You have to consider if your dial witch project could go gray."

"I'm a white witch."

"Who, like all other white witches, can make mistakes or be led astray."

"Why can't you just believe in me?"

Cassie firmed her mouth. She wasn't going there. "I

could ask you about your services, but I'm guessing you're in the planning stage."

"I've had a vision. The rest will come." Jane turned her sketch pad back in her own direction and continued drawing. "What have you been up to?"

"Chasing leads on Larry's murder."

"Ooooh." Jane put down her design. "Tell me more."

Cassie's shoulders relaxed. It was good to have family to talk to. "First, tell me what happened to the men?"

"Your men? Living or dead?" Jane winked.

"Saucy brat." Cassie glared at her.

"The dead one is still sleeping, if that's what they call their dead state. Sometimes you really have to tell me about your relationship with him. I mean, what's it like to do the deed with a stiff? Stiff, right? Get it? The man with the popsicle."

Cassie rolled her eyes.

"Okay, okay, I'll stop." Her sister grinned. "But, how's his stamina."

Cassie shook her head in disbelief. Did Jane have any filters? "Let's just say, I don't recommend vampires."

"Not even for one night?"

It would be a long one, she thought, but didn't say. This was her little sister. "No. definitely not. They can be ..."

"Addicting?"

"Yes," Cassie admitted. "You could say that. "And dangerous. Remember, they are always dangerous."

"Sounds sexy to me."

"Of course, it does. But no, don't go there."

Jane tilted her head. "Be honest. What you really want to know is what happened to one very much alive, wicked warlock?" Jane grinned. "The one who has a thing for you?"

Cassie rolled her hand, indicating she wanted her to spit it out.

"He fumed."

"Fumed?"

"Seriously. As soon as he found out you had left the building without telling anyone where you were going, he fumed."

Cassie stifled a laugh. "What did that look like?"

"First, a deep purple mist swirled around him. Peregrine appeared and with a nod teleported out of the room, to Goddess knows where. Then, get this. He drew a pentagon on the living room floor, entered it, drew a circle of power around it, and began muttering."

"What did he say?"

"He kept his voice too low for me to hear. But a crystal ball appeared in his hand, and he looked into it."

"And you just watched?" That didn't sound like Jane.

"I wanted to get closer, but he had bound me. I couldn't move."

"What? He bound one of us? How dare he?"

Jane giggled. "Actually, it wasn't' so bad. I like how he likes you so much he's willing to break all the rules."

Cassie shook her head. "What happened next?"

"He looked me straight in the eye and said, 'Tell her to behave herself,' snapped his fingers on both hands, and vanished."

Cassie laughed. "He does have a way with exits."

"That he does." Jane swept her long red curls behind her shoulders and leaned in. "Tell me what you've been up to."

"Well, like I told you, Larry, a friend of mine, was shot dead in an alley."

"Yeah, yeah. The homeless guy."

"I've been following leads. I just found out about two

suspicious strangers coming to town."

"Are you going to tell the hot cop?"

"No, I promised my source I wouldn't. But let me tell you about my suspect list."

Jane leaned in. Sid jumped up onto the windowsill, and stretched her long body out to soak in the sunshine. Her eyes closed in bliss.

"First, there's Ava, an older woman who lives on the street. She says she's normal as long as she takes her meds. But I'm not so sure of that." Cassie laughed. "People think she's crazy because she sees shadows and Martians."

Jane smiled. "But she could be seeing one of us."

"Exactly. Anyway, Ava was a friend of Larry's and has told me about his other friends. She's a good source."

"Okay, who else."

"I talked with Father Jacob, the priest. Now there's someone who looks like the walking dead. He let Larry sleep in a back room of the church in exchange, for doing some cleaning chores. At first, I thought his feelings for Larry sounded real, but he sweats when I talk to him, and he doesn't have an alibi for the time of his murder. He's got secrets. I'm sure of it."

"Who else did you talk to?"

"A guy who goes by the name Kit, short for Kitilano where he used to live. He sleeps in the alley doorway of the main bakery in town, and sometimes with a lady friend. He gave me the most information."

"Keep going. I bet you've learned more than you realized. Talking it out might help."

"Well, Kit was by all accounts, a good friend of Larry's, and at the time of his death Kit was with a cocktail waitress by the name of Melinda Goodtimes."

Jane chortled. "You can't be serious."

Cassie threw up her hands. "That's what he said. Hey, maybe you could check her story out for me. She works at the Rusty Anchor bar and has a room above it."

"I'll check out his story. I've got to find out if Goodtimes is her real name. What else have you learned?"

"A city-slicker by the name of Reaper is suspicious. I saw him hanging out with my friend Ronnie, the mayor. She's a witch, so I can ask her more about him. Also, there have been two strangers dealing drugs in town and they've been seen at the church."

"That's a lot of leads."

"That wouldn't stop Jessica Fletcher. I'm going to chip away at them one by one."

"Why not throw the hot-cop a few."

"Mmm, no. Let's just say, he's not as good as I am at questioning suspects."

"But he has other resources," said Jane.

"That's true," Cassie said. She reached for her phone.

Gavin answered her call after one ring. "Are you okay?"

"Never better." She lied.

"Are those men still at your house?"

How much should she tell him? "Listen. I'm having coffee at my kitchen table with my sister. Catching up, and we got to talking about Larry."

"Uh-huh. Still playing amateur detective."

"Listen. Did you know a business man by the name of Reaper? He's new in town."

"Reaper," Gavin repeated.

"Do you know him?"

"I know who you're talking about. He's planning on starting a business here, and he's been asking around about empty buildings and properties. If you think there's something sketchy about him, I'll find out more." He paused. "Do

I need to give you my lecture about leaving murder investigations to the pros?"

"Nope. Of course not. I just happened to hear about this guy, and I thought you would want to know."

"Uh-huh. Why don't I believe you?"

Cassie spelled her phone to create static and ended the call. "Men," she complained. "Why do they always want to lecture me?"

"Because they actually believe you'll listen to them," said Jane.

Cassie smiled at her sister. "It's good to have you here."

"Good to be here."

"I'll leave you to your business plan. I just have one question."

"Okay. Let me see. If I had to pick between the vampire, warlock, and human cop..." Jane grinned, "I'd choose all three."

Sid meowed. "A wise woman."

"That wasn't my question, but thank you for sharing your unwanted opinion on the matter of my love life. I was wondering if you knew anything about the search for Brianna."

"Oh, that." Jane frowned, and the freckles on her face paled. "A warlock sends texts back to Sanjay every three hours. The posse is tracking down every lead they have, but so far—no luck."

"How could a simple kitchen witch evade a posse of supernatural beings with an assortment of skills and abilities?"

"If Erebus is backing her, she can go anywhere, do anything." Jane said. "Erebus is more powerful than ..."

The line hung in the air for a minute.

"Then all of us put together," said Cassie.

TWENTY-TWO

"May your coffee kick in before your reality does."
~I love Coffee meme, FB

Becoming a sidekick to an amateur detective didn't light Jane's broom stick on fire. But wanting to help her sister, Jane headed straight to the bar to check out Melinda Goodtimes. It had to be a stage name, she thought. Vixen, always at her side, giggled.

The old, wooden saloon was built on stilts at the end of the main dock. It had a faded mural painted on its side and rotting steps. A cedar sign hung above the entrance read, The Rusty Anchor.

A petite woman with large breasts strode out of the doorway and stopped a few feet away. She pulled a package of cigarettes out of her apron pocket. Had to be a waitress, thought Jane, probably the late thirties.

"Hey," Jane said.

The woman exhaled a plume of smoke. "Hey."

"I'm new in town," said Jane.

Silence followed, but it wasn't an unpleasant silence.

More like a calm after a storm. Vixen sauntered over to the edge of the dock to lay in a shaft of sunlight. She stretched herself out and settled in for a nap.

Jane lifted her chin. "I'm visiting my sister, Cassie Black, and I'm thinking of staying. My name's Jane."

The woman turned towards her with a faint smile. "Cool," she said. She needed a perfect brew, or two, and a brow treatment. Her long blond hair had been pulled up into a sad-looking bun, and she smelled of greasy French fries, beer, and Black Orchid perfume.

"I'm liking it," said Jane.

The woman exhaled. "It's a good town," she said.

"If you like clouds," Jane said with a smirk.

"Yeah. You gotta like rain." The woman inhaled deeply, as if her life depended upon it, and exhaled. "It cleanses the soul."

Jane let that comment hang for a few seconds. "Hey, do you know Melinda Goodtimes?"

The woman dropped her cigarette and crushed it hard with her worn boot. "I've been called that. What do you want."

"Uh. How do I say this?" Jane sighed. "You see, my sister's been asking around about Larry's murder." Jane looked up at a seagull squawking above her. She wondered what the odds were of getting pooped on.

"Yeah I heard she's been asking around," said the waitress.

Jane tore her eyes away from the bird. "I'll get right to the point." Before that bird does something. "Kit said he spent the night of the murder with you, and Cassie wants to take him off her suspect list."

The woman's hazel eyes turned harder than marbles. She tilted her head back and laughed. "You're as subtle as a hammer, you are." Her raspy voice gave her words a gravitas, revealing her street savvy.

"Look," said Jane, "you can clear Kit's name. Was he with you, or not?"

"Yeah, he was with me. All night." She gave a wicked smile. "Do you want details?"

"Nah. I just wanted to be sure Kit is in the clear." The seagull stared at her from his perch on top of the sign. He wiggled his bum, and Jane spoke faster. "Do you have any idea who killed Larry?"

"That's a hard one." The woman took another drag on her cigarette, and Jane noticed her long, fake fingernails. "I figure some stranger did it. Everyone liked Larry. He was a nice guy, you know. No one around here would hurt him.'"

"I wish I could have met him," said Jane forcing herself not to look at the bird. "Cassie's grieving hard."

The waitress nodded. "We all are."

"Hey, if you hear anything about the murder, please, let us know at The Brew."

"Okay. I'll do that. I don't like cops, but I like your sister. She gives stuff to the homeless. If I hear anything, I'll get the word back to you."

"Thanks."

"And by the way, my name isn't really Goodtimes."

Jane's cheeks burned.

"It's Melinda Shneidersky. Only Kit calls me Goodtimes."

Jane laughed. "Got it. I'm sorry if I offended you."

"No worries. You can call me Mel. Want to come in for a beer? You don't have to worry about seagulls inside." She smirked.

"Next time," said Jane. "I've got stuff to do."

As soon as the woman turned towards the bar, Jane vanished herself out of town.

WITHIN SECONDS she and Vixen landed at the Lookout, a viewpoint high on the cliff above the town. With her sleepy cat at her heels, Jane walked along the trail to the picnic area breathing in the fresh salty air. With a snap of her fingers, she covered a picnic table with a freshly-ironed, red-and-white-gingham table cloth, and a full service for high tea with two plates.

Vixen purred and sat on the table. Jane poured herself tea and put scones, cream, and lemon curd on both plates. Vixen drooled.

Two seagulls appeared overhead, and Jane shuddered. They're everywhere in this town, she thought. An omen? Hard to say.

She raised her hands and holding them about a foot apart grew a vibrant-cobalt-blue, ball of energy. It glistened with sparkling light. "Protegas me puppi deturbat ab avis," she chanted, 'Protect me from bird poop.' She threw it in the air, and it spread above the picnic area like the top of an umbrella. When it stretched to a perfect size, she clicked her fingers, and it became invisible.

Jane sent a text to Cassie, "Melinda Goodtimes confirms Kit's alibi."

Cassie replied. "Awesome. Thanks." Followed by a happy face emoji.

That's enough work for today, thought Jane. "Time for tea," she said and sat down. After a sip, she spoke. "Being one of the younger witches in the Black family has its advantages and disadvantages, Vixen."

The cat, used to her witch rants, simply chewed.

"There are advantages. Most of the heavy lifting gets done by my older sisters, and all the great expectations of my parents are placed on their shoulders. That leaves me ample opportunity to have fun." She exhaled noisily.

Vixen's whiskers, coated in cream, twitched.

"The disadvantage is that no one takes me seriously, or at least not as seriously as I deserve."

Vixen's tail thumped.

Jane took a bite of her buttery scone slathered in lemon curd and whipped cream. She chewed slowly, enjoying the flavors and textures of what she considered to be the most perfect food in the universe, next to potato chips. She swallowed. "You know, I mastered all the basic spells and potions by the time I was ten. Ten! I'm a kick-ass psychic and an empathetic healer. But they, the royal they, think I'm nothing but trouble wrapped up in a pretty package."

Vixen padded over to Jane and put her soft paw on her face. "I know, dear one. I know. The life of a young witch is difficult." Her breath smelled of the sardines she ate for breakfast.

Crunch. Crunch. Crunch.

The sound of someone approaching on the trail caught Jane's. She strengthened the protections spells she wove around her body, and readied for battle. In this town, anything could happen. Or at least that's what Sanjay had told her.

A man broke through the bush ten feet away. And what a man! He had to be at least six-feet tall, with a slim build and a mop of thick, unruly black hair. His dark blue eyes shone with excitement as if she was the best ice-cream sundae he had ever laid his eyes on. Energy buzzed all around him.

Jane licked her lips. He reminded her of someone.

"Oh, hi,' he said. "I'm sorry if I startled you." His eyes scanned the tea table and then returned to her. Mischief danced across his irises.

Jane felt naked. "I was just having a pity party with my cat. I do that sometimes," she said.

"Yeah, me too." A crooked smiled crossed his face, and she knew who he reminded her of. "But I don't see a cat?"

That settled the supernatural question. Vixen had made herself invisible, but if he had any magical powers, he would have been able to see her. "You don't look like a cat guy," she said.

"No. I prefer dogs. But right now, all I can afford is a goldfish."

She nodded sympathetically. "Shh. Don't say the f word in front of my cat. She gets kind of crazy when she hears it."

Vixen jumped down, ran into the bush, and reappeared in a visible state for the sake of their visitor. She tilted her head and squinted her eyes at him, presenting her best dumb kitty look.

The man gave a good-natured laugh and walked closer to Jane.

His seductively woodsy scent made her toes curled.

"My name is Brody Buchanon. You gotta be new in town. I've never seen you around here. And I wouldn't miss you. No one would miss you."

Jane couldn't help but smile. Another man could say the same thing and sound cheesier than cheddar, but this guy spoke with a down-home sincerity that charmed her to the bone. "Are you related to Gavin, the cop?"

His crooked smile reappeared along with dimples to die for. "Yeah. He's my cousin, the first son of my mother's brother. There's actually a lot of us around here. It's impossible to go a day without running into someone in the family."

"My name's Jane Black. I know all about big families. Your cousin threw me in jail, by the way. Would you like to join me for tea?"

"Black, eh?" His eyes twinkled, and he folded his long body into the bench of the picnic table. "Let me guess you like coffee."

"Among other things," she said. "How do you like your tea?"

"Hot."

That did it. Jane liked him. Just the right amount of playfulness, mixed with country charm and respect. Why didn't she wear her lucky bra today?

"Because you were spending the day with me," said Vixen in her head.

Jane took Vixen's plate and gave her a brief but spectacular, evil eye, as she passed it over to Brody. "Do you like whipped cream?"

Vixen rolled her eyes.

Brody's boyish grin turned positively devilish, and he paused before he said anything. "Sure," he said at last.

But the damage was done. Jane laughed and tossed her long red curls over her shoulders.

BRODY WONDERED what he had got himself into. He had come to the Lookout to clear his head. Everything in his life was screwed up. Heck, as he drove up on his motorcycle, he had even considered jumping. That's how messed up he had become. But then he met Jane.

Whoa. Just whoa. Women like her only existed in fantasies. She was so hot. Really hot. Tall, slender with a dancer's build. Long, curly red hair and green eyes that shone in a magical way. And she was so friendly. It didn't bother her to meet a strange guy in the woods. She showed no fear or even sensible caution. Was she mentally challenged? Hell, maybe he should worry. Gavin had put her in jail. He squirmed in his seat as she passed him her cat's teacup.

"I met Ophelia, once," he said.

"Really? She was my great aunt, but I never met her. I only heard stories, and they were wild. Tell me, did she dance naked with you?"

Tea spurted out of Brody's mouth.

Jane laughed again. She didn't laugh like other women. Not a tee-hee sort of thing. She laughed with her whole heart, and it pulled him in. Big time.

"She had to be in her seventies," he said, wiping his mouth with his sleeve.

Actually, she was over a hundred, thought Jane, but she didn't say that. "I was teasing you," she said to Brody. "But, you know, she was known in our family for having a wild lifestyle that included music, men and dancing. The age of her men never bothered her."

"I wouldn't know about that. I made Ophelia a sign for The Perfect Brew. That's how I met her. She seemed like a really nice, old lady."

"So, you're a painter?"

He shrugged. "No. I'm a mechanic at the garage, which is owned by another uncle of mine. I'm apprenticing there. It's good steady work, but greasy. I make signs as a side-gig."

"A side-gig? Fascinating." That's what she had been thinking about. It's funny how life sends you the information you need when you need it. And in such an excellent package, she mused.

"What do you do?"

I collect bird feathers for potions, read tarot cards, and experience visions, she thought, but she didn't say that. "I just finished college, and I'm thinking of starting a business."

"Cool." He heaped lemon curd and whip cream on the scone she passed him. "What kind of business?"

A witch business, she thought. "I'm not sure. I'd like it to help people."

"Like social work stuff?"

Jane took a bite of her scone. "Sort of."

"There's no money in that."

"I think there's a market for what I can offer, and life's not all about the money, anyway. I'd say my project is of a cross between being an Ann Landers and a social worker."

He chewed slowly. "So, what's stopping you?"

"Well, number one is my family. They'll think I'm crazy." They always do.

Brody shrugged. "That's no reason to stop. You gotta do your own thing. What else is stopping you?"

Jane put down her scone. He was right, of course. Why couldn't she have seen that for herself? Well, maybe she did, but hearing someone else say it gave her more confidence. "I don't know how to run a business."

"It's not hard. You'll need to make a webpage, open a bank account, and do some advertising."

"You seem to know a lot about it."

"Our family has several businesses in town. Uncle Gregor runs the winery just north of town. He makes a great Cabinet Savignon. Uncle Ian runs the garage I work in, and it's been said he's the best mechanic on the coast. Aunt Emma runs Mystic Esthetics, the biggest beauty parlor in town, and Aunt Millie runs an accounting firm that does everyone's taxes. Gavin becoming a cop, was an exception to the pattern. I've helped in all the family businesses my whole life."

"My family keeps busy, but running small businesses isn't the sort of thing they do." They preferred to work on creative projects. She took a sip of her tea. "You seem really smart about this stuff. Would you help me start my business?"

Brody leaned back. His denim-blue eyes darkened. "Uh, I would love to, but there's one problem."

Jane would fix that problem. "What is it?"

"My fiancé wouldn't like it."

Jane felt her chin drop, but she recovered it quickly and pasted on a smile. How had she so misread the guy? He didn't look taken. "Maybe if I spoke with her," she said.

GAVIN LICKED the lemon sauce off his upper lip and shook his head. No matter what he said, he knew he would regret it. The universe screwed him over again. His life sucked so bad. He put his cup down and stood. "Nice to meet you, Jane. I liked your biscuits." Had he really said that? So, lame. "I'm glad Gavin let you out of jail."

Jane stood. "It was nice to meet you, Brody Buchanon. I hope we meet again."

TWENTY-THREE

"Coffee makes us severe and grave and philosophical." ~ Jonathon Swift

Sanjay sat in his favorite leather chair by the window in his turret. In his right hand, he held a martini. On his lap he held a template with a map on it. Peregrine perched on the chair opposite him, staring out the window at the changing sky, as dusk descended quickly on the drizzly, gray day.

"Mapping wards encompassing the town is tedious," Sanjay said, "but it has to be done. We can't be overlapping spells and wards in one area and leaving others vulnerable. We must be efficient with our magic. An appropriate balance must be struck. Otherwise, all manner of disruptions in our lives could result." Not to mention the universe, he thought.

"Just because something has to be done, does not mean it has to be done by you." Peregrine shuffled his feet. "I understand you decided to become a responsible warlock. I even admire that in you."

"But?" Sanjay glared at him.

"But paperwork Sanjay, my dear warlock, it is beneath you. Beneath us."

The warlock chuckled. "I suppose I could train someone to do it, but it would have to be a witch, warlock, or sorceress who understood wards, the portal, and the importance of secrecy."

"And who doesn't mind paperwork," grumbled his bird.

Sanjay took a sip of his drink and puzzled that thought. "Perhaps, Gabriel?

"Donovan's son? I do like him, but he's a bit young, don't you think?"

"He's sixteen. His magic is strong. I trust him. He would enjoy being part of the inner circle in town. I will offer him mentorship in his magic and a steady fee. I'll ask his father for his approval, of course."

"No warlock would refuse you. Not even Irish." That was the name the bird used when referring to Donovan O'Reilly. Peregrine rotated his neck. "Shall I keep an eye on the boy? Make sure he is worthy?"

"Excellent idea," said Sanjay.

Peregrine flew through the closed window and vanished into the night sky.

THE AIR SUDDENLY COOLED, and a fissure of energy rippled thought the room. As Sanjay stood and raised his hands for protection, he found himself facing Alessandro. The blood sucker had to be at least a foot taller than himself. Without women around to temper the vampire's demeanor, the guy looked meaner than the devil himself, like a warrior ready for a brutal battle. The kind of man who get off on violence. Dead meat, Sanjay thought.

"What the hell do you want?" Sanjay asked the vampire.

"To talk to you, obviously," said Alessandro.

"How dare you invade my home without my permission." Sanjay's fingers moved in preparation for a dramatic show of magic.

"Relax, warlock. I don't need a light show. I came for our mutual benefit."

Sanjay glared at him.

"Your wards are strong," the vampire added. "I searched for an opening and could find none. Then I got lucky. When your familiar slid out, he disrupted the net long enough for me to slide in."

"I'll fix that."

Alessandro nodded his approval.

"Is it fair to assume you don't want me dead?" asked Sanjay.

The vampire chuckled. "If I wanted you dead, warlock, you would already be dead." He grinned showing off his teeth. "But we both know that such a kill would be problematic for me."

The warlock folded his arms. "What do you want, vampire?"

Alessandro nodded slowly and grimaced. "Have they found the woman who poisoned Cassie?" he asked.

"Brianna. No. Donovan O'Reilly, a trusted friend, and talented warlock, is overseeing the search. I hope to hear news soon."

"Do you want vampire reinforcements?"

A nice offer. "Not yet. But if you could have your people listen for word of her, that would help."

"Consider it done."

The vampire continued to stare at him. The hair on the

back of Sanjay's neck rose. He put his hands in his pockets and clenched his fists. "Is there anything else?"

"I know you have feelings for Cassie," said Alessandro

"How I feel about Cassie is none of your business." The words came out faster and tighter than Sanjay had wanted.

"She's mine." The vampire's voice thundered.

Sanjay smirked. "I don't think she sees it that way?"

Alessandro chuckled. "No, of course not. She would say she is her own woman, and that no man could ever own her." He grumbled. "But that's just modern female crap. Let us talk like men. Cassie's mine. She is destined to be mine, for now and for eternity."

Sanjay's throat tightened. "And, you think I'm standing in your way."

The vampire's nostrils expanded. "Women are temperamental. I find patience is the best weapon to use against them. It takes time, but I have all the time in the world."

Sanjay felt his brows rise. Weapon? "Hmm," he said.

"Cassie is going through some changes and needs her space," the vampire said. "I understand that. The death of her great-aunt shook her up, and she wants to find Larry's murderer. She has a big heart, and she wants revenge." Alessandro walked further into the room and sat on Peregrine's chair. "I also get that she needs friends. I may not like it, but it's a fact."

Sanjay sat in his own chair. "Relax, Alessandro. We aren't in the kind of friendship you're worried about." Yet.

The vampire nodded. "I sensed that. You have not yet bonded."

Sanjay clasped the armrests of his chair. Diplomacy had never been his forte. "Can you get to the point." Bloody bloodsucker.

"I have a business to attend to in Amsterdam. I know I

can't talk Cassie into coming back with me. I came to ask you to protect her."

Sanjay leaned forward. "You're asking me to take care of her?"

"Yes."

Sanjay scratched his chin. "You know she has magic, formidable magic of her own, that is growing by the day."

"What I know is that she is stronger with you by her side. As much as that pains me to see. You have combined magic that is ..." the vampire paused, "significant."

Significant? Of course, Sanjay knew this, but the fact the vampire could sense it surprised him. Had he sent spies? Heard things? The warlock cleared his throat. "So, let me get this straight. You want me by her side as her protector, but you don't want me to become her lover. That's what you came to tell me."

Anger lit Alessandro's dead vampire eyes. "She is mine." He hissed.

"You already said that."

"You are a friend she will soon forget. Trust me. Lovers with beating hearts are forgettable."

And yet the vamp wanted one for himself. Unless ... unless the sucker intended to turn Cassie into his own kind. Forget that. Sanjay fought his emotions to keep them off his damn face. "Alessandro, keep your fangs in. The way I see it, we have a mutual concern, the safety of Cassie."

The vampire nodded.

"I will protect her." As long as she lets me.

"And you understand that she is mine." The ferocious hiss returned, and the lights in the room flickered from the vampire's anger.

"I understand you want Cassie to be yours, and if that is what she wants, I will not stand in your way."

The vampire's dead eyes narrowed. "What do you want from me?"

"I want you to promise you won't turn Cassie without her permission."

Alessandro's fangs emerged, glowing in the light. "I could say yes, but we both know vampires lie."

Sanjay smiled. "And you know warlocks are sneaky."

TWENTY-FOUR

"Coffee: The favorite drink of the civilized world." ~
Thomas Jefferson

After Alessandro left, Sanjay had much on his mind. Top of the list: Would the blood sucker take Cassie against her will and turn her? His kind weren't known for kindness, and clearly Alessandro felt possessive. There had to be spells to protect her from such a fate.

Peregrine flew in and mounted the back of his chair. "Aren't you getting ahead of yourself."

"What do you mean?"

"The vamp isn't stupid. He's going to figure out you've already taken his woman's heart. What then?"

I wish, thought Sanjay. Cassie was interested in him, of that he was sure. But she wasn't his. Not yet. The idea of being with Cassie, making her his, felt undeniably right. "I'll look for spells to protect us both."

Peregrine rolled his eyes. "You're a goner."

A flaming message arrived and Sanjay grabbed it from the air with his right hand. It could mean only one thing.

The Brotherhood had come to a decision. He swallowed. If the court believed him and found in his favor regarding the matter of rescuing Brackenfeld's wife, then Sanjay would become one of them again. There would be a big brew-haw ceremony with lots of magic, but he could handle that. He clenched his jaw. Yeah, it would be a bit a broom-and-chain relationship all the way, with lots of expectations that would bristle his butt, but he had no choice. They would help him secure the portal and protect Cassie, and for that matter the world, from Erebus.

If the court ruled against him, he would remain a renegade warlock with only his wits to fall back upon.

He read the note:

SANJAY KAHN,

You are reinstated as a member of the sacred warlock brotherhood. A ceremony in your honor will be conducted six months hence on the full moon.

Magic Prevails,

Grimshaw

Council Chairman

SANJAY GRINNED. "I'M IN."

He spent the next three hours sending carefully constructed fire messages to Anton Wizenhall, the chief historian of the Brotherhood, a mage of great repute. Sanjay requested information about Erebus, the high court, Puer Dei, poisons and protections from vampires. There was so much he needed to know, and now he had the best library on magic at his disposal. Sometimes the Fates smiled upon him.

As he sat back in his chair, filled with gratitude, he detected the distinct smell of Fishermen's lozenges. His nose twitched.

George floated into the room. George Caraway was the original owner of the house who had been poisoned by his mistress for his money. A short plump man in life, he was even shorter in death. He wore the blue and white striped pajamas he had been wearing the night he died, with his initials embroidered on his right breast pocket, GC. His rounded jowls, a deathly shade of white, wobbled. His eyes were sunken black orbs, in folds of what had been skin. He sucked on his phantom cough drops as he stared at Sanjay.

"Mr. Kahn," he said.

"I'm busy George. Go haunt another room."

"You let the undead into my house. I must object."

That was an hour ago. Sanjay scratched his head noting it took the ghost a long time to muster the courage to appear. The vampire's presence must have opened the door for him. "George, the blood sucker is gone. I promise to strengthen my locks, so he can't return."

Silence.

"George, I'm busy. Please, go away."

A fire message appeared. Ignoring his ghostly intruder, Sanjay read it out loud to Peregrine.

"REGARDING EREBUS. You didn't need to waste my time for this question. You could have found him on Witchypedia. Erebus is one of the primordial deities born out of the void, Chaos, the personification of darkness and shadows. His siblings are Gaea (earth), Eros (love), and Nyx (night.) I suggest avoiding him."

Magic Prevails,

Anton."

Sanjay winced. Nothing new there.

"You should ask them about recent sightings," said Peregrine.

George rose above them and moaned. "Nooooo. Nooooo. Noooooo."

"What's wrong with you?" asked Sanjay.

"You can't bring the Lord of Darkness into my home."

Sanjay counted silently, aiming at ten, and made it to two. "George, you don't know what you're talking about. I am writing a paper and needed information. That's all. I am not about to call upon primordial deities in my home."

"My home," said George as he touched the window shutters and made them rattle.

"George stop it. You're not scaring me, and you're dislodging dust."

"Master, would you like me to peck at him?" asked Peregrine.

Sanjay smiled, remembering just such an incident that happened on the day they moved into the estate house. "Later," he said as he grabbed the next flaming note, and read it out loud.

"REGARDING THE HIGH COURT. It is a council of 9 elders (descendants of the original 9) who oversee the welfare of all the dimensions. They have their own language, called elder."

HMM. Stormy had been honest and accurate, thought Sanjay as he grabbed the third flamer and read it.

· · ·

"REGARDING the subject of the Puer Dei. It is a Latin term that translates to "child of god." Our libraries have several books on the subject. My general recollection, having read these texts years ago, is that we are all children of god, but there are those among us who are more closely aligned. Their vibrations are more attuned to the light. Such individuals are referred to as being Puer Dei."

GEORGE SAT in the windowsill of the turret and moaned. "Mmmmmm. Mmmmm. Mmmm."

Ignoring the ghost's bad manners, Peregrine said, "So, you believe Cassie is Puer Dei?"

"Stormy said she is, and it makes sense."

"But she's a lousy witch."

Sanjay nodded. A smile spread across his face. "I have a theory about that."

"Oh great. Another theory." Peregrine scratched his wing with his beak.

George continued to moan.

"Suppose," started Sanjay, "just suppose you wanted to protect someone who had special talent, until they needed to actualize their full faculties."

"Eeeevil," moaned George

Sanjay waved a dismissive hand at the ghost, and ignored him.

"You would hide her." Peregrine said, shifting his feet. "You're suggesting her inability to use simple magic was a cloak to hide her true potential."

"Which are coming alive." Sanjay paced the room. "Cassie is only beginning to understand her true powers. Every day since her inheritance her magic has become stronger."

"And Erebus wants to kill her, because of her powers."

Sanjay turned to look at his bird. "I can't pretend to know how darkness thinks, or if he thinks. Perhaps he works on instinct. She is light. He is dark. And so the story goes." Sanjay scratched his chin. "He wants unguarded access to the portal and sees her as someone in her way."

"Eeeevil," moaned George as he rose in the air and sat in the rafters. "Eeeevil, will haunt you."

Sanjay looked up at him. "You can moan all you want, George. This is my house. If you don't behave, I will banish you again."

Peregrine chuckled. "You're getting soft, master. Where are your lightning bolts?"

Sanjay narrowed his eyes at his familiar. As always, the falcon told the truth. In his younger years, he would have vanquished the ghost. But not now. George had no other home to go to, and Sanjay felt badly for him. He looked up at the fat apparition. "George you can hang from the rafters all day, but you have to know it won't do you any good. We're not scared of you."

"You should be," George's voice echoed through the house. "You should be scared. Very scared."

A fourth flame appeared and Sanjay read it.

REGARDING VAMPIRE PROTECTION SPELLS. Officially we have a pact with the Vampire League. They won't fang us, if we don't spell them. That being said, vampires love to break rules. We know of only one spell that works on them. It is not something we would trust to the messenger service, however, so you will have to pick it up on the full moon.

Magic Prevails,

Anton.

p.s. We are analysing the poison you sent us. It is a doozy.

SANJAY WALKED over to his chair. George pulled the chair from under him and he landed on the floor with a thud.

The ghost cackled.

TWENTY-FIVE

"Our culture runs on coffee and gasoline. The first often
tasting like the second."
~ Edward Abbey

Sanjay entered Cassie's apartment through her window, pushing aside the wards she had placed on it, as easily as a cat swishes items off a counter top with its tail.

Cassie sat at her desk typing on a laptop. Without turning she spoke. "Don't tell me it's you."

"Who else would it be."

Sid sauntered over to the warlock and jumped up onto his shoulder to welcome him with a loud purr. At least someone in the family loved him.

"I put up two new wards!" Cassie said.

He scratched Sid under her chin. "Yes, I noticed that, but I put one up first, so that any wards added on top of it won't keep me out. Kind of like Teflon."

Her anger heated the room and not in the way he wanted. "Cassie, relax. We're on the same side," he said. Why couldn't she be reasonable? Oh yeah, she's a witch.

"Hmph." She turned to glare at him. "I like my privacy." Venom burned in her eyes

"I get that. As soon as you are safe, you can have as much privacy as you wish. But until then, you can forget about acting like a caged prissy princess. I am guarding you whether you like it or not." How did she get under his nerves so quickly? "

Cassie scrunched her lips and grumbled.

He took a deep breath. "Especially now."

"What?" She stood and folded her arms. "What do you mean, 'especially now'? What happened?"

"I had a chat with your dead lover-boy."

Her brows rose. "I'm sure that wasn't pleasant."

"Actually, it didn't go as badly as you might think. He wants me to watch out for you."

She blinked. "Seriously? He asked you to protect me?"

Sanjay nodded.

"So, Alessandro left?" she said.

"Yes. He has business to attend to in Amsterdam."

"I am not his property. Just so you know."

Sanjay nodded.

"Nor am I yours."

He nodded again, but thought, 'not yet.'

Cassie stepped closer. "We're clear on that."

There were so many things he wanted to say. Perhaps, should say. But the words weren't coming out of his mouth. They stuck in his head. Should he warn her, that Alessandro planned to turn her? Did she already know? Should he tell her how he really felt about her? Did he even know how he felt about her? He cleared his throat. "I've been re-instated in the Warlock Brotherhood."

She squinted. "I'm happy for you. I guess." Her eyes

turned a psychic shade of green. He hadn't seen her do that before. "That is what you wanted. Isn't it?"

"Yes. Now we can access the largest library on magic that exists," he said. in a matter of fact tone.

"Any news on Brianna?"

"Not yet."

"So you're my personal witch-sitter? Here to watch me?"

He stepped closer and slowly placed his hands on her shoulders. The last thing he wanted was to upset her enough that spelled him with her wonky magic. "I'm here," he said. "Please, don't take offence. I'm here to tell you to stay put. Forget about searching for murderers. Forget about the coffee business downstairs. Forget about showing Jane the town. Just stay put."

"Stay? You're ordering me to stay. I'm not a dog. You can't force me to stay."

"I'm not forcing you to do anything." Though heaven and earth knows, I would love to. "I would never force you to do anything." He hesitated. "Unlike a certain blood sucker threatened to ...."

"Don't go there," she warned. "I'll sort my vampire problems on my own."

Okay, then. He had never heard her sound so angry. "Let me explain my situation, before you get all hexy," he said. "I want to help with the search for Brianna, but I can't do that and guard you at the same time. I need you to be safe." He swallowed. "All I'm asking, is that you stay in your apartment. There are enough magical wards on this place to keep out Erebus, or any army of evil beasts that do his bidding."

Cassie looked at her nails, painted a sexy red. Gently, he brushed a silky tendril of her hair out of her face. Everything about Cassie was so womanly, and her scent made him want to grab her and take her away, but he couldn't. "I get it. I'm sorry I barked at you. Barked like a dog. Get it?"

She made a face and stifled a laugh. "Sorry. I shouldn't be so bitchy. I know you mean well. I don't like being stuck in here. I appreciate all you're doing for me, and I promise I'll stay out of trouble."

Hmm. Cassie said the words he wanted to hear, but did she mean them? Not in the slightest. Something in the pit of his warlock gut said, NOPE. Loudly. "Cassie, please."

"Sanjay," she said in a seductive tone.

Her eyes flashed a dark jade green. Again, not something he had seen before. Her body inched closer and his, hardened in response. Maybe, if they just kissed once. He leaned towards her.

"Sanjay, we can't."

Witches!!! There's a reason their name rhymes with bitches. He frowned. Did her voice sound sad? Maybe, a little. If she knew how he felt, how he truly felt, would her response be different? Or, maybe she loved the dead guy. "Hmm," he uttered.

She traced her fingers along his face and his whole body lit on fire. "When things settle down," she said. "We should talk."

"Settle down?" he muttered. "Do you mean after we find Brianna? Or after we expel Erebus from this world? Or after I get the vamp to stop sniffing around you?"

Cassie rested her head in his shoulder and his arms pulled her closer. She fit so perfectly. He buried his head in her hair and held her tight.

Sometimes silence said more than any words ever could.

TWENTY-SIX

"Coffee ... Smells like magic and fairy tales."
~ Lacie Pinnell, FB

Jane sat opposite the loan officer at the Mystic Keep Bank, fluttering her eye lashes as if she had an insect lodged in them. The man was middling in all respects. Middle aged, middle height, middle weight ... middle looks. He had introduced himself as Mr. Shnit and given her a limp handshake. She guessed him to be about forty, but he could be younger. His coke-bottle glasses and dandruff-riddled suit, made him look more boring than her Latin teacher, and that was saying a lot.

Ignoring her batting-lashes and every other part of her, he stared at her application, which lay before him on his desk. As he read through it he made little snorty noises. Shnit the snorter, she thought. To distract herself, Jane looked around. The sides of his small cubicle, dotted with yellow sticky notes perfectly lined in rows, looked efficient, but again boring. She stifled a yawn. How long could it take to read one page?

His beady eyes looked up at her. "You want the bank to loan you money to start a new business."

"Yes," said Jane in a perky voice. "Yes, please," she added, hoping it might help.

"And you list your needs as: Website fees, Hookup fees and a cool Van."

"Yes," she said. "Yes, exactly." At least he wasn't dumb.

"Mmmhmm."

What kind of answer is that? She watched him reread the document.

He frowned. "Well," he said, "the amounts for the website and internet seem reasonable." He snorted and continued to read.

"I checked on them this morning," Jane said. "They are the most current costs."

"Mmmhmmm ..." He tapped the fingers of his left hand on the desk. "Mmmhmmm."

"Is there a problem?" she asked.

"Not with the numbers. No, not with the numbers. Your addition is solid." His beady eyes looked directly at her. "I wonder if you really need a van."

"I love vans," Jane started, ready to explain to him all the things she could do with one.

He held up his right hand. "That's immaterial. As I said the figures overall are acceptable."

Jane squirmed in her seat. "Are you saying, something else is unacceptable?"

"Not sure. Not sure at all," he said and snorted.

She squinted to read his name tag, so she wouldn't get it wrong. "Mr. Shnit, I don't understand."

"I've never met anyone who wanted to open a business like this."

Jane firmed her lips. Of course, she had expected some

concern. People had difficulty understanding her creativity. But she had arguments ready for him. She knew, with certainty, that this business would work. It would be profitable and it would help the community. It was as if everything in her life had led to this moment. Besides, she had seen it all in a vision. It was her destiny. The universe was about to open up and grant her this.

He pursed his pruney lips. Not a good look. "Let me get this straight. You want to open a business modelled after the 1-300-I-Got-Junk organization."

"Yes. Exactly." She hadn't written that down, but the banker had read between the lines. A good sign.

"Only yours will be called, 1-300- I Got Witch?"

Jane sighed. Her ideas for the business had bubbled within her ever since she had the vision, and she had had no one to talk to about it. Every time she brought it up with Cassie, her response was a lecture on being responsible. "I can help people in so many ways. Just so many."

"I admire your enthusiasm, Ms. Black."

Oh-oh. That was never a good comment, and one she had heard many times in her life. "I read in the Financial Times that the most successful businesses have three things in common." She used her serious voice, which felt as comfortable as a sweater made of itchy wool.

He looked at the wall clock in the distance, and steepled his hands. "Go on Ms. Black."

"One. They offer a product or service that helps people. The more authentic and helpful the item the better the profits. I can so nail this one."

The banker's bushy brows twitched. She needed to sound older.

"I guarantee my services will help and never harm." It was the essential part of the white witch oath, after all.

Before he could interrupt her, she continued. "Two. They have a positive and healthy company culture. I can guarantee this too. I will do all the work myself. I may need to hire some jobs out, like advertising but I like people and I'll make sure that I'm extra nice to all my associates. People like me." She beamed her best smile, the one that opened doors and hearts.

Meanwhile a gaggle of twitchy butterflies danced in her gut. She really wanted him to approve this loan. Her alternatives were going home and working on some dumb family project, or asking her father to back her. Neither appealed to her.

Mr. Shnit glanced at his watch. "And number three, Ms. Black?"

"That's the best part. The most successful businesses offer something no one else does, or offers a similar thing, but in a unique way. Trust me, my service is unique."

"I see," he said with the most uncommitted voice imaginable. "And tell me again what your service is?"

"Magic."

"I see. I'll be blunt." He looked around as if he expected people to be listening in. "Are you a hooker, Ms. Black?"

Jane's mouth dropped. "No!. Oh, my goodness, no. It's not about sex." She hesitated not wanting to lie, because witches were often asked for love potions and virility enhancers. "Well unless. No. It's not. It's about wish fulfillment." Maybe, she should spell him.

He steepled his hands again. "Wish fulfillment," he repeated.

Swallowing the acid rising in her throat, she continued. "You see, people want things in life. They need someone to talk to, to sort out their feelings. I'm going to be that person."

"But you don't call yourself a life-coach or a councillor. You call yourself a witch." His whole face twitched.

Jane had promised herself not to use magic to get this loan. She wanted to tell her father she had used her business sense to get what she wanted, and she had persuaded a bank to back her. She bit her bottom lip. How much of the truth should she share? The countless lectures Cassie had given her about hiding her abilities in this town flowed through her mind.

"Mr. Shnit, helping people comes naturally to me. I've been doing it all my life." That was true. "I am so good at what I do that I have been called an angel, and I have been called a witch." True. She paused. "To call my business "1 – 300 – I Got Angel" just wouldn't be right, to my mind. It's almost blasphemous, because I'm not an angel." By any account. "So, I thought I'd use the word witch. People will take notice of that word and when they start using my services, news of my good work will spread quickly." She leaned back, exhausted.

"But, Ms. Black, to promise magic is dangerous," he said.

"Only if you can't deliver," she said, wishing she could convince him. "Is there anything I can do for you, Mr Shnit?"

The color in the banker's face drained, and he stood. "Ms. Black, it has been very nice to meet you, but I'm afraid at this time the Mystic Keep Bank cannot assist you. I don't see 1-300- I Got- Witch as a viable investment."

She pleaded with her eyes.

"I recommend you work on a solid business plan and change the name."

Jane dropped her head in her hands as if she were crying. It gave her a minute to close her eyes and stretch her consciousness into his, exploring his mind. She wouldn't make him do what she wanted, but there were other ways she could persuade him. Other ways.

Unaware that his essence was being probed by a skilled sorceress, he gave her a sympathetic look, and passed her a tissue. "There, there, Ms. Black. You are young..."

Raising her head, Jane fixed him with a witch's stare.

The banker's body trembled and he stammered. "It's time for you to, Ms. Black."

Jane stood. "And you, Mr. Shnit. I'll bring you the business plan tomorrow."

Before he could say more, she vanished. Walking to the entrance of his cubicle, he looked around, and she simply wasn't there. She wasn't outside either. How could that be? Could she be a witch? Perish the thought. Witches don't exist.

Or do they? A voice deep inside him, chuckled, and it sounded amazingly like Ms. Jane Black.

TWENTY-SEVEN

"In Seattle you haven't had enough coffee until you can thread a sewing machine while it's running." ~ Jeff Bezos

Sanjay caught up with his friend, the warlock Donovan O'Reilly, at the Keep. It had become the unofficial headquarters for the search. The stone structure resembled a fortified tower built by European nobility during the middle ages. They used them as safe houses when enemies took over their main castle.

The Mystic Keep stood as a sentinel high above the harbor. It looked like a lighthouse made of old worn stones and had a storied past that included lingering old magic.

A rookery of cormorants perched on its balcony. To the uninitiated the Keep felt cold and forbidding, but to mages it felt like home. O'Reilly had created a pattern of wards around it to protect their meeting. Only those invited could enter.

Sanjay walked through the arched doorway, and climbed the spiralling wooden staircase to the second floor. Water ran down the inside of the stone walls and the air smelled musty, but inside the room a large fire crackled and the air smelled like the forest on a spring morning.

The room was lined by five narrow windows, but little light came through them from the gloomy day. Outside, dark clouds scuttled across the sky, blocking the sun. The air had turned cold. Waves crashed against the cliff as the wind picked up. A storm was gathering.

Inside the leaders of the search party gathered around a circular table. O'Reilly wore warlock fighting gear, over ripped jeans, and a white tee-shirt covered with a protective vest. He was a tall man with a warrior's build. Black hair framed his face, dominated by brilliant blue eyes. Strapped to his body he had a gun, bow and numerous knives edged with deathly spells. He sat closest to the windows, ready to guard against intruders.

Gathered around him sat three supernaturals in their human forms. They were the leaders of the teams who hunted Brianna. Sanjay nodded at the group and took a seat at the table. Peregrine stood on guard in the window sill. They all nodded back at him, acknowledging his arrival.

"Reports," requested O'Reilly.

Hank Henderson, a gargoyle with a reputation for strength, rose first. In his human form he stood seven feet. Muscles bulged beneath his battle fatigues. If he were a car, he would be a Hummer, thought Sanjay, who had not met him before this day. A gnarly, battle scar ran from the edge of his right eye down his face to his neck. His aura read loud and clear, 'Don't mess with me or mine.' He spoke in clipped precise words like a military man. "My team of warriors searched the ground. In the first hour we located faint markings of her footprints on a forest trail. They led to a cliff high above the ocean. We found nothing else. It's possible she jumped." He sat down.

Pussy Nip, a werecat with a reputation for being an exceptional stalker, rose. A lithe woman who wore black spandex well, she had the hard-black eyes of a murderess. Her aura spoke of deadly-ends, and made Sanjay's personal wards shiver. Her ebony hair had been carefully braided and wound around her head. Magic concealed her weapons around her athletic build, but he could sense them: an assassin's toolkit. She lifted her head high. "My team of shifters searched the canopy. I thought I smelled something wicked, but wasn't able to catch up with it." She hissed her dissatisfaction and sat down.

Normally just being in the same room with the werecat would get a rise out of Sanjay, but not tonight. He ran a hand over his face. Peregrine whispered in his head. "You're a goner."

Last, but far from least, stood Zatara of Xanadu, a sorcerer who was known for his knowledge of arcane spells. Being adept at magic it was impossible to gage his age. His white hair had been pulled back into a ponytail, revealed a wizened, but handsome face with stormy-blue eyes that changed in tone with the color of the sea. "My team of mages traced her movements, scrying in water and crystal balls. We haven't located her yet." He looked around as if weighing his audience.

"It's most strange," he continued. "Every so often we found a wisp of her essence, but never in a stationary position and never moving in a tangential manner. It was most frustrating." The fine muscles on his face tightened. "And it worries me." He paused. "Deeply."

They waited. It being not wise to rush such a powerful and dangerous sorcerer. Peregrine shifted from foot to foot

"I suspect," Zatara said at last, "someone sprinkled bits of her around to make us run in circles."

Sanjay's gut clenched. "That would mean ...."

"Yes, warlock," said the Zatara the sorcerer, "that would mean Brianna is no longer alive."

"Hmm," said O'Reilly. "That means we chased her ghost."

In the distance lightning cracked through the dark sky and the rumble of thunder vibrated in the Keep.

TWENTY-EIGHT

"Starbucks says it's going to start putting religious quotes on coffee cups. 'Jesus! This cup is expensive!'"
~ Conan O'Brien

Cassie promised Sanjay she would stay safe, and she intended to. But she had no intention of stopping her detective work.

"Your dick work?" Sid smiled at her own joke. "Get it dick, as in private dick."

Cassie nailed him with as withering a look as she could muster. "Larry's murderer has to be brought to justice," she said.

Sid rubbed against Cassie's leg to express empathy. Or maybe it was just a cat thing, thought Cassie.

"My dick work, eh?" she said as she reached down and scratched behind Sid's ears. "I like that." Cassie picked her up and with Sid in her arms magically whisked them into Ophelia's attic room. With a click of her fingers she lit all the candles. Next she removed the clutter on the old, oak desk, and moved her aunt's grimoire it into a drawer.

"Huh," said Sid.

"Yeah, I know. Right? I'm getting better at magic."

Ophelia's crystal ball was the only thing left on the desk. With a snap of her fingers, sage burned on the altar at the side of the room. "I call on the power of earth, water and fire. Clean this space. So,mote it be." Dust zapped into oblivion, faint odours left by past spells vanished, and papers flew around the room finding their place.

"Interesting," said Sid with only one eye open. She shook her body as if a bucket of cold water had been dumped on it.

"Get used to it," said Cassie. "This is the new me." Hardly believing the truth in her own words, she shivered.

She sat in the desk chair to scry with the crystal ball. It was the size of a small bowling ball, and made of rose crystal. "It's beautiful," said Cassie wanting to touch it, but not daring to do so.

It had been created by ancient magic at least a century ago. She knew from the academy that if she tapped it, it would sing a high-pitched note only people of magic could hear. Knowing something and experiencing it were two different things. Summoning up her courage she tapped it lightly and felt the vibrations moving in the room.

Cassie had looked at the crystal ball every time she visited the attic room. She had felt it calling to her from the first moment she laid eyes on it, and it had become a mysterious presence in her life, sometimes haunting her dreams. But she had never dared to touch it before now. Fear of the unknown, coupled with poor witch-esteem had held her back.

Erebus was coming, and she had to use all the magic power she could access to fight him.

As she picked up the crystal, an awareness ran through

her. This orb no longer belonged to Ophelia. It was now hers, an extension of herself. Shocked by this realization, Cassie almost dropped it.

Crystals had never called to her before, and this one claimed her.

Sid pawed her leg. "Don't hold back. Stormy said your powers would grow."

"That she did," said Cassie.

The vibrations in the orb grew. It hummed and grew warmer to the touch. This was the energy conduit to a larger consciousness. a highway of awareness that binds all living beings. Cassie swallowed and put the crystal ball down.

Sid jumped up cn the desk. "Go for it, Cassie."

Cassie bit her lip. Could she handle this advanced magic? There was only one way to find out. She cleared her mind. Dropping all her worries and thoughts, she stretched her consciousness and centered her energy. She lifted the crystal ball into her hands again. Combining her magical energy with that of the orb should, in theory, create a portal to the larger essence of being. It should allow her to see anywhere, and in a sense, be anywhere.

But would she have control over the process? What if she got lost and a demon took control of her? Maybe she should have another witch with her. As her fears swamped her mind, she put the orb down again.

"Trust yourself," said Sid who pawed the air. "The ball is calling to you. That means, you are ready.

Okay, then. Cassie picked it up and cleared her mind. "Ball, show me what you will."

It glowed nicely, sort of like a night light. But nothing happened. No sparks. No smoke. No mirror. After all that worry—nothing happened. There was no song or dance or even a stink. Cassie groaned.

She had attended crystal classes, and she knew adept witches could see things in the silent orbs. Of course, that had never been her experience. Her father gave her a crystal ball from Witchmart on her sixteenth birthday. That was her first. She had held it, talked to it and spelled it as best she could. After three hours it burst into flames for some unknown reason. She claimed it was defective and exchanged it for a cashmere sweater.

Since then she had been given two crystal balls. The experience always ended in flames after little progress. Her mother said she needed to temper her energy. Whatever. Cassie had given up.

"But now you are in Mystic Keep," said Sid. "And your role as Pur Dei is beginning."

True. Supposedly. So why not try again? Crystal balls were used all over the world to reveal the past, present and future. Some believed they pulled images from the collective unconscious. Others said the images came from the practitioner's subconscious or imagination. Some believed gods, spirits and/or demons were involved in the process. People made simple magic so complicated.

Crystals amplify the mind. That's all. It's as simple as that. The source was the source of all. Some liked to call that source a God or Goddess. Others simply call it consciousness.

To tap into the magic of the crystal ball would be amazing. But did she dare? Sanjay had offered to mentor her on the craft, but she had refused as it would create one more link with him. She could ask Jane to help her. Jane was good at all things magic.

Sid rolled her eyes and thumped her tail. "Get on it

with it, already."

Yeah, the cat was right. It was time to witch up. Cassie closed her eyes, opened her mind and willed the crystal ball to come to life.

And nothing happened.

She peaked through her right eye. Still, nothing. Well, at least it didn't burst into flames, she thought.

Pressing her eye lids together, and hoping with all her heart, she whispered to the universe,

"I call to the north, the south, the east and the west,
Bring this crystal to life.
So mote it be."

She peaked through her left eye. Nothing.

There had to be a way.

Clunk. Clunk. Clunk.

What was that noise? She looked towards the source. The grimoire drawer glowed with a blue light. Huh! That had never happened before.

She opened the drawer with an incantation and her aunt's spell book flew through the air, plunked down on the desk beside the crystal ball, opened to a page. Cassie read the title of the page, "Scrying with Bob."

"Bob?" Sid chuckled.

The crystal ball glowed brighter. Cassie scanned the page and the next and the next. There were ten pages of instructions on how to converse with Bob. Several incantations were listed for various activities, and Ophelia had detailed how to create more. How had Cassie not seen this before?

"Magic reveals itself when you are ready," said Sid, repeating one of the mantras from her academy.

Cats are annoying, thought Cassie.

"And you weren't ready," said Bob, the crystal ball.

Sid's hackles rose. "Bad, Bob. Bad, Bob. Bad, bad Bob."

"Shut it, cat," answered the glowing globe.

Eye of Newt! Cassie ran a hand through her hair. Of course, she would inherit a crystal ball called Bob who would argue with her snarky familiar. She let out a breath she hadn't realized she held and started laughing. She couldn't help it. Sometimes life became too ridiculous to be real.

"Reality is only in your head," said Sid who was also in her head.

Bob snorted.

A crystal ball that snorts? Good grief. Shouldn't communing with a ball be a mystical experience? She needed to control him. Running her fingers down the open page of the grimoire, she stopped at the incantation titled, "For a Wider View," and read the spell out loud.

Bob's globe became translucent. "Tell me more," he said in a saucy voice.

"Show me Ronnie's last encounter with Reaper."

Bob appeared cloudy for a minute and then his surface cleared. Within the ball, Cassie could see Ronnie sitting beside Reaper on her office sofa.

"Bob, let me hear what they're saying," Cassie commanded.

"If you insist," he responded in a bored voice.

"RONNIE," Reaper said. "I swear, the green streaks in your eyes flicker like magic in this light. You're positively bewitching." His beady black eyes roved over the mayor's hourglass figure lingering here and there.

"Mr. Reaper, this is a business meeting." Ronnie's voice sounded unusually cool.

"Call me Lucas."

Ronnie's eyes narrowed. Cassie knew her to be a talented, clairvoyant witch, and Cassie could only guess what Ronnie was seeing in his mind. "Lucas," Ronnie said slowly, "you said you wanted to talk to me about investing in my town. So, talk. I'm a busy woman."

He leaned in. "Your town has potential, Mayor."

Her perfectly manicured right brow rose slowly. "Potential for what?"

"Investment. I like what I see, and I think ..." he leaned closer ... .

"Oh, no." Ronnie pushed him back with her palm. "I'm not easy pickings. Nor is my town."

He grimaced.

She waved her hand in the air, and a fine blue mist rose from her skin. "Tell me exactly why you're here," she said.

His skin turned an ugly shade of purple and his form shook as if a mega-earthquake hit him. "Witches," he grumbled. "The town is filled with witches and other magic folk."

Ronnie tipped her head to one side. "That doesn't really bother you does it?"

"As long as they stay out of my business."

"I see. You're part demon. Your expensive cologne cannot hide the stench of evil that oozes from your skin."

"And, you're full witch."

"What exactly is your business?"

"Importing and exporting. I need a safe place to base my operations. You have an adequate port and a quiet setting. If the supernaturals agree to stay out of my way, I will give the town ten percent of my profits."

Ronnie stood and walked to her office window that overlooks the main street "Ten percent?"

"I estimate it would be at least a million dollars a year to start and it would grow from there as I develop a network along the west coast."

She turned back towards him, and a smile spread across her face. "You say a million, but you thought ten, and planned to hide nine. Be careful when you deal with me and my town."

He growled like a wounded bear. "I'm prepared to offer you a million per year, and if my profits rise, I will increase the amount."

"And my town can use this cash any way we wish?"

"Of course."

"Imports and exports, you said." She walked closer to him, holding her arms loose at her sides ready to draw magic.

"You don't need to know more," he said.

"I understand. You assume your investment guarantees you privacy."

"Yes," he said.

"I'm prepared to accept your offer, Mr. Reaper."

"Good." He stood up and reached out for a handshake.

She stared at him. "On one condition."

He pulled back his arm. "Name it."

"It has nothing to do with the drug trafficking."

His eyes rolled sideways so that only blackness filled the orbs, a movement common to demons who have lost control. "Get real, witch. Drugs are everywhere. You can't stop the flow of them. Junkies cause their own despair."

"I don't wish to argue with you. Let me be clear. I have no intention of encouraging the drug trade. Now, I'd appreciate it, if you would just leave. I have work to do."

"Two million."

"No," said Ronnie.

"Three, and that's my last offer."

"Mr. Reaper, the problem is not the amount of money you offer. It's the nature of your business." The mayor walked over to her desk and sat down.

He growled. "Madam Mayor, if you won't take money, I'll find another way." He stomped out of her office and slammed the door behind him.

With a click of her fingers, Ronnie cleansed the room. But the stench left a trace and the mayor looked worried.

BOB SPOKE UP, " Have you seen enough?"

"Uh," Cassie hesitated. "I may need you in a few minutes. I have to think first."

"Uh-huh," said Bob. "I bet that's hard for you."

"Bob,"

"Yes, mistress."

"Shush it."

Cassie had wanted to swear, but the words stuck in her throat. She needed the crystal ball to work with her. Insulting him would be stupid.

"But it would feel good," said Sid in her head. "Let me do it, next time."

"I need to think," Cassie said.

Bob grumbled.

"Mr. Reaper is a drug dealing demon who wants to use the town as a home base," said Cassie. Had he already been dealing in town? That's the question she needed to answer. Did the two strangers work for him? Did he know the priest? She had a lot to learn about the demon.

TWENTY-NINE

"If I asked for a cup of coffee, someone would search for a double meaning." ~ Mae West

Cassie wanted evidence so badly her teeth hurt. There was no way in hexin'-hell she could go to Gavin and tell him about Bob.

Larry must have stumbled across a drug business at the church. She guessed that's where the two strangers stored their stuff, and Reaper was probably their boss. The puzzle pieces fell into place. Larry must have seen something that put him in danger, and that's why they shot him. If she shared her theory with no credible evidence, Gavin would think she had gone bonkers.

Sid chuckled.

Cassie gave him the stink-eye.

Sanjay would have a warlock, hissy-fit if she left The Perfect Brew, but she itched to get to the church and see if she could find something. The drug dealers had to be stopped and the murderer had to feel the hard edge of justice.

Jane came out of the guest room with her sketchbook in hand. "Wait till you see my logo designs. No one will be able to resist my business." She plunked the book on the kitchen counter in front of Cassie.

Cassie rolled her eyes. "Dial witch?" She had hoped Jane would let that idea go.

"Yeah. It's catchy, right?"

"It screams, I am a witch."

Jane nodded. Cassie sighed. "You know we're in hiding, right?"

A smile beamed across her sister's face. "Not for long."

What? Cassie shook her head. Little sisters could be such a bother. "I don't have time for this right now."

"Still trying to catch a murderer? Hmm."

Cassie sighed. "I've figured it out, but I don't have any proof."

"Cuz the big, bad warlock wants you to stay safe at home." Jane's eyes lit up with mischief. "I get that. I like the guy, by the way. Mostly, I like how much he liiiikes you." She poured water into a French Press. "Don't worry. I can look around for you, like before."

Cassie told her about Bob. After Jane stopped laughing, Cassie said, "I think Reaper and the two strangers run drugs out of the church. Larry found out and was killed because he knew too much."

Jane closed her eyes and wiggled her nose. "What can I do?"

"Can you watch the church? If the two strangers show up, follow them. I'm going to use Bob to follow Reaper. Sooner or later the three of them should meet. I'd like to be a fly on the wall at that gathering."

"You're working with a crystal ball!" Jane's eyes

widened. "And nothing's blown up? Should we take out extra insurance?"

Cassie rolled her eyes. "Bob and I get along just fine."

"You are full of surprises."

"Will you help me out?" Cassie asked.

"I'm on it. Just tell me what the men look like. I'll text you every thirty minutes with an update." She saluted. "If I don't send a message, send Stormy or someone to find me."

Tension rolled off of Cassie's shoulders. "This could work," she said.

Jane smiled. "I like being your sidekick. Does that make me a side-dick?" She laughed at her own joke.

"Okay, let me describe Reaper and the two dealers." She licked her lips recalling Ava's descriptions. "The head guy Reaper, a soul-sucking drug dealing demon who uses a lot of hair products to mask his evil scent. His two helpers I've never seen. According to Ava one is tall and walks with a limp, and the other is short, stalky and bald."

"Limpy and Baldy," repeated Jane.

A knock on the door stopped their chatter. "Are you expecting anyone?" asked Jane who walked towards the door.

Cassie shook her head.

"Police, let me in," announced Gavin from the other side of the door.

Jane laughed. "Can I have this one?"

Cassie wiggled her finger and a sofa cushion flew through the air to her sister's head. "He's too much of a cop for you."

Jane stopped the cushion mid-launch. "But he likes kissing witches. Or so I heard."

"Just open the door."

Jane opened it, smiled at the officer, and walked past

him. "See you later, Cassie," she yelled over her shoulder. "Have fun with Bob."

Gavin walked into the living room and turned towards her. "Whose Bob?"

"No one," Cassie said. "Come on it. Would you like a coffee?"

"No thanks. I spent the last three hours drinking downstairs."

"Are you guarding me, detective?"

"I was listening for information. You can learn a lot from the conversations of coffee drinkers."

Cassie winced as she thought of her clientele and all the possible chatter he might have overheard. She felt a light headache coil between her eyes. Hopefully the supernaturals had been careful. "Did you hear anything useful?"

Gavin had a way of owning a space. He strode into the kitchen area and took a seat at her table as if it was something he did regularly. "Let's see. Your friend Stormy started knitting a new pattern. Her friend Mabel is upset with her hairdresser because she no longer buys the right magazines. Oscar has a hot date tonight with a blond woman with mile long legs and six figures. The rest of the baristas say it will only last a night." He paused. "I could go on. I have a great memory for detail."

Cassie laughed. "An interesting job you have."

"Yeah. It's a ball of fun. I'm glad to see you haven't left your apartment. Is that because the tall pale guy told you not to move, or was it Sanjay's doing?"

Cassie sighed. "Everyone told me to stay put. I chose to do so, because it makes sense. Have the police found any leads on Brianna?"

"No. I'm sorry. Not yet."

"I don't understand why she would want to hurt me."

Gavin pulled a notepad out of his inside pocket. "How well did you know her?"

Cassie groaned. Her cell phone beeped and she picked it up. It was a text from Jane. 'At church. Nothing to report.'

"I know," said Gavin. "You don't want to go through this again." His deep, cop voice brought her back to their conversation.

"I know it's your job to keep asking me the same questions, but it really is annoying." And a colossal waste of my time. Didn't you say you have a good memory.

He put down his pen and leaned forward. "Then let's talk about us."

Us? Oh no. "Uh. I thought we had decided there is no us."

He took her hand. "I lied."

"About what?"

"I think about you."

Her cell phone pinged. Another text from Jane. '2 perps headed into church. Will follow.'

"Oh no," Cassie said out loud and then put her hand on her mouth.

"Yes, Cassie, I do. From the first moment I saw you, I felt bewitched. There's no other word for it, and when we kissed ..." He sighed. "It wasn't like kissing any other woman. You captured me, if that makes any sense."

Sid purred.

Cassie stood. "No, I didn't mean 'no' to you. I mean I do mean 'no' to you. A definite 'no,' but that's not what I'm saying."

Gavin pulled back. His eyes narrowed. "What are you saying?"

"Jane could be in trouble. Please, if you care for me at

all, go to the church. Right now. Gun drawn. The whole cop bit."

Gavin's jaw twitched. "That makes no sense. What trouble could Jane be in? There aren't any fire hydrants in the church." Seeing Jane's empty mug on the table, he poured himself a cup of coffee from the French Press.

"You want me to say it, don't you?"

"What?" His brows made a deep V.

"We're witches. Okay. We're witches. The kiss was a humdinger, but part of the hum you felt was because I am a magical being."

His mouth dropped. "I suspected."

"Of course, you did. You're a good detective and," she paused, "an awesome kisser, but right now I need you to help me protect Jane."

"This is a lot to take in."

"Give it time. But right now, help Jane."

"Did she mess with bikers again?"

Cassie took a deep breath. Gavin was a good man, of that she had no doubt, but could she trust him to do the right thing?

"Talk to me, Cassie."

"I believe there is a drug ring in town, run by a man called Reaper. He has two main lieutenants and they run the drugs through the church. Larry knew something about them and was killed for what he knew."

Gavin's cop face took over; hard, analytical and energized. "And Jane?"

"I sent her to follow the two thugs. I just wanted her to watch them. But you know Jane isn't one to just watch the circus."

Gavin swore. "If she's a witch can't she just wiggle her nose and protect herself."

Cassie swallowed. "Yes, but that may not be enough against Reaper."

"He's a witch? Or do they call boy witches warlocks?"

"He's a demon, the kind no supernatural wants to go against."

"And you want me to take him on?"

"If Jane stays on sacred ground, he can't do too much to her. If you can get to her before she's stupid enough to follow them out of the church, all will be well. If she follows them out onto normal ground anything could happen."

"Anything?" He said slowly. "Should I take special weapons?"

"Your gun will slow him down." She waved her hands in the air and focused her energy on a silent spell. Mist grew from the floor and spun.

"What the hell?" Gavin took a step back.

A shining dagger appeared in the mist. Cassie grabbed it, said another silent spell, hexing it to fight demon energy and passed it to Gavin.

"Wow," said Sid in her head. "You, the witch who couldn't boil water, created a demon dagger. That's high-high-level magic."

"My sister is in danger," Cassie said out loud. "And so is the town."

As Gavin lifted the weapon into the air, magic crackled along its edge and slid into his arm. He bowed towards her. "I will protect her."

THIRTY

"...a cup of coffee, black as a moonless night, hit the spot." ∼
Twin Peaks

As the door closed behind Gavin, Cassie received a new text from Jane. 'Hiding behind a pillar watching. The two thugs are talking to the priest. I need to get closer to hear what they are saying. He looks like he's in a trance.'

'Gavin is on his way. Stay safe,' Cassie wrote back. Safe? Jane? That was an impossible request.

"Call the warlock," said Sid as she jumped on the table to look Cassie directly in the eye.

"He's busy."

"Call him."

Cassie closed her eyes and concentrated on Sanjay. ' I need you," she whispered.

A swirling fog of silver mist formed in front of her and the warlock materialized. In one hand he held a sword high in the air, and in the other he held a revolver at chest height. His body vibrated with magic. "Cassie?"

"Jane's in trouble." Cassie's eyes welled with tears of emotion.

"Where?"

"The church."

He swirled his arms creating another portal.

"Wait. Let me explain." But it was too late. Sanjay had vanished.

NOW A SENSIBLE WITCH would gather her wits about her and make a grand plan, but no one had ever called Cassie sensible. As she teleported to the foot of the church's stairway, she considered how she would handle the demon and his drug ring. There weren't enough stairs to come up with an answer, so when she reached the top she flung open the door and walked straight in. Indiana Jones never had a plan, why should she?

The priest stood behind the lectern at the front of the long room, looking like one of the walking dead in a B-movie.

He looked at her. "What now, Ms. Black?"

As she walked up the aisle she rattled off questions in her head. What do you know about drugs in town? Do you know the two strangers? Was Larry connected with drugs? How does the church feel about drug dealers? Is the creeper Reaper a friend of yours?

"Well?" he said when she reached him without saying a word.

"I've heard rumors," she said.

"About?" His voice held no charm.

"Two strangers in town have been coming and going from the church. No one seems to know much about them." She paused, but he simply stared at her as if she had lost her mind, so she continued. "There are more drugs in town, since their appearance, and I was wondering ...?

He closed his bible. "I too have been wondering," he said.

That just didn't sound good.

"Of all the things found on heaven and earth..." he paused.

That sounded even worse.

"The vilest among them is the witch."

Cassie didn't see that one coming. She called her magical power from every cell of her body and focused it in her hands preparing to defend herself, but not quickly enough.

He threw a glass of holy water at her, and when it didn't burn as he must have expected, he recited a spell, "Ipsum revelare, malefica," reveal yourself, witch.

Cassie forced herself to laugh. "I am not a black witch," she said, and holy water won't hurt me because I am not evil."

"But you are a witch."

"Where is Jane?"

"You are both witches."

She put her hands up in surrender. "Okay, okay. You're right. We are witches, but we are good witches and practice magic only to help people."

"Goody, goody-two-shoe-witches. Blah." The priest made a retching sound. "If you knew what was good for you, you would leave town."

"Where is my sister?"

From the back hallway, Reaper appeared pulling Jane by her hair. A dark aura above his head pulsated with violent thoughts. He threw Jane forward and she fell to her knees. A dog collar had been placed on her swan-like neck and he held the chain attached to it. "Is this who you're looking for?"

Jane's eyes were bloodshot. Her skin looked paler than a vampire's. It took all of Cassie's strength to not run to her. She had to be careful for both their sakes. "What have you done to her?"

The demon laughed. "Not much. Yet. But I have plans. Many plans." A wicked smile spread across his face. "Your sister is young and so luscious."

Thunder rumbled in the distance and the walls of the church shook.

"Let her go."

"She knows too much. I cannot let her go."

Cassie sensed the men before they came towards her. The two strangers. Not the party she wanted.

"I promise, on my honor as a witch of the Black Magnolia coven, we will not reveal your secrets, if you just let her go."

Reaper laughed.

"Boss, we can get quite a lot of money for a pair of sister witches on the market, especially two as pretty as them."

"Later, after I am finished with them." With a wave of his hand, the ceiling closed in on them and the lights turned to blazing pits of fire. The air smelled of charcoal and death. The sound of millions of people screaming filled her ears.

Cassie shook her head trying to clear it. She had to keep her senses. But her magic was no match for this demon from hell.

He laughed, and his thugs laughed, and the priest fainted and fell into a heap on the floor.

Focusing all her magic in her right hand she raised it and pushed her palm towards Reaper. "Stop this madness," she screamed.

"Or what?" A flame burst from the floor a foot in front of her and circled her.

"Or what," he repeated. The flames grew higher.

Cassie raised her second hand and closed her eyes. She prayed to all that was, all that is and all that would ever be, to give her strength and clarity. If ever she needed her magic to work this was the time.

"I call to the north, the south, the west the east,

Stop this darkness, stop it now.

Let the light return

So, mote it be."

The wailing of lost souls stopped. Cassie opened her eyes. The demon stood a yard in front of her. "Is that all you've got?" He snickered.

She pulled on her magic again and slammed it at him with the palms of both her hands. Light crackled in the air between them. Lightning bolts flew at his neck.

He raised his arm and blocked them. "Anything else?"

The sound of a police siren in the distance buoyed her confidence.

Cassie stomped her foot and kicked him in the shin as hard as she could.

"Ow," he said, and smiled. "I like difficult women." He stepped closer.

"Get away from me." The stench of dark alleys, fetid streams and decaying matter oozed from his skin, making her stomach roil. This could not be her fate.

"By the time this night is through, I promise you, you will want more of me." He hissed and his eyes turned into burning flames as he reached for her heart.

Gavin ran through the front door at full speed with his gun pointed at Reaper. "Don't move," he ordered.

With a flick of a wrist, the demon turned Gavin's gun

into molten steel and the detective dropped it. "What the ...."

"You aren't invited to the party," Reaper said to him.

Gavin kept running.

"Don't," yelled Cassie.

He passed her and threw himself at the demon, who stood placidly waiting for the assault. At the last instant Gavin pulled the demon dagger from his belt and plunged it into the monster. They both tumbled to the floor.

Reaper had jumped to the side at the last moment to save his heart, but the magic laced weapon caught him in the leg as they fell. He screamed in agony, the piercing screech of a wounded animal.

Out of a swirling silver portal Sanjay leaped into the room and slay Reaper in the heart with his warlock sword.

The demon snarled. His hand rose in the air to cast a final spell. But the white magic coursing through him pulled his hand down. The warlock stood above him.

Jane moaned as she returned to consciousness, and Cassie ran to her side. Her pulse was stable, but her eyes had a shocked expression. Cassie squeezed her hand and put her jacket over her.

The two thugs ran for the front door, but Sanjay with a flick of his wrist locked it. "Sit down in the last pew." He ordered.

Gavin stood and walked back to the two dealers. "What's happening to my town?" he mumbled as he took handcuffs from his belt.

"They have no power," said Sanjay in a matter of fact voice. "They only had the power bestowed on them by the demon, and he can no longer help them. Treat them as normal criminals."

"Scumbags," Gavin muttered. "Drug dealing scumbags." He read them their rights and cuffed them.

Cassie joined Sanjay standing over Reaper. The demon's body ignited into a fire and he melted into the floor leaving a patch of slime and his distinct stench behind.

For a too brief moment Cassie locked eyes with Sanjay, and a feeling of calm flowed through her. They had done it.

Gavin walked the dealers to where Sanjay and Cassie stood. He said to the criminals: "You have something to tell us?"

The tall one took one look at Sanjay, whose face was still in warlock-commando-mode, and started talking.

"Reaper hired us to run drugs through the church. Some heroine and weed, but mostly fentanyl. Business was good."

Jane got up and wandered over to the priest. She took his pulse, and shook her head. He probably died of a heart attack, thought Cassie.

She turned her attention back to the thugs. "Did you know Larry?" she asked them.

Sanjay scowled at them, which made the taller one twitch, and the shorter one look away.

"One night he caught us moving a shipment," the bald man said.

"I chased him down and shot him in the alley, twice for good measure. I've never killed anyone before. You gotta believe me. It was Reaper. He messed with my head. It felt like he was inside me. Killing seemed natural."

"Was Father Jacob part of this?" asked Gavin.

The man crossed himself. "He didn't want to be. But Reaper could be very persuasive. It was like he took over your thoughts."

"You always have a choice," said Gavin.

Cassie exchanged a knowing look with Sanjay.

Gavin looked at Sanjay, and for a minute Cassie thought he would say something. Instead, he nodded with respect and ushered his prisoners out of the church.

"Did you hex Gavin?" Cassie asked Sanjay.

"Didn't have to. You kissed him. Remember?"

"Huh. Good one." Cassie punched him gently in his abdomen. "Why did it take you so long to get to the church?"

Sanjay's marmalade eyes blazed with latent power that hadn't yet settled. "I was here, by your side, the whole time. I waited for the best opportunity to kill the demon. That's how warlock's fight." He brushed a strand of hair from her face. "It was hard not to jump in sooner, but I knew if I waited for the right moment we would have a better chance of surviving this. I would have sacrificed myself before I let you die. You must know that."

Cassie smirked. "You had a plan. That makes sense. Unlike me, the witch who rushed in and was making a mess of it."

"I didn't say that."

"You thought it." How could he not?

"No, I didn't think that. I don't know what you've got against warlocks, but I wish you would see me for who I am." He paused. "See us for who we are together." He lifted her chin and looked deep into her eyes."

She could barely breathe.

"You blew me away," he said softly. "You were so brave and courageous and ..."

"Stop it already," said Jane, walking up to them. "Just kiss her."

THIRTY-ONE

"I am pieces of all the places I have loved. I've been stitched together by song lyrics, book quotes, adventure, late night conversations, moonlight and the smell of coffee."
~ Brooke Hampton (FB meme)

Cassie took a step back and looked towards the altar. She wanted that kiss more than she had ever wanted any kiss in her life, but not here in the place where they had vanquished a demon, and not now, in front of her little sister who would undoubtedly post a photo of it on social media. As her vision settled on the holy dais an odd awareness crept into consciousness.

"Who's there?" she called out.

Sanjay and Jane looked around and then back at her.

"Someone else is here," Cassie said.

Jane stood next to her, closed her eyes and grabbed her hand. "I feel it too. Sanjay seal the doors."

"Done," said Sanjay, who drew his sword still wet with the demon's blood and gore. He took a warrior stance and scanned the room

Cassie trembled. Someone was there, but she hadn't a clue what to do about it. It couldn't be, or it shouldn't be Erebus, as they stood on holy ground. As she tried to make sense of her feelings, Jane spoke out.

"Reveal yourself spirit. Tell us what you have to say."

Sanjay spelled the room with a Sanskirt incantation, purifying the space. Sparks of purple light crackled through the air.

The image of a person materialized in front of them, a ghostly spectre. As it took shape Cassie saw a woman with long hair. The scent of tangerines filled the air.

"I am sorry," the spectre said.

"Brianna?" asked Cassie.

"Yes, it is me." Her voice sounded distant and distorted. "I'm sorry. So sorry. I didn't want to hurt you."

"The darkness took over your soul." Sanjay said in a matter of fact voice that anchored the emotions in the room.

Brianna's image became clearer. Her edges more defined. "I thought, I could handle him. I've made deals with demons before. Little things, you know. An exchange of spells that benefited both parties and hurt no one. But this time, I went too far. He gave me my biggest wish, and in my moment of weakness I didn't consider what he would want in return. I should have asked. When the time came, he took over my body and I poisoned you. I did it both times."

Cassie walked closer to her. "What did he give you?"

"He cured my father's cancer."

"I didn't know your father was ill," said Sanjay who made it his business to know about all his employees at The Brew.

"I didn't tell anyone. The pain was too great, and there

was nothing anyone could do. The doctors had given up. They told us to say our final good byes."

Cassie winced. "How did the darkness know all this?"

"Erebus knows everything," said Sanjay. "That is the way of evil. It knows our weaknesses. Knows how to manipulate us. I wish, Brianna, you had come to me first."

The ghost nodded. "He appeared to be a regular, lower-class demon. You have to believe me. I had no idea I was dealing with Erebus."

"You knew he was dark," said Jane.

Cassie gave her sister a stern look. Brianna felt badly enough.

"No, Cassie, your sister is right. I played with evil, and I should have known better. He told me the special coffee brew I sent to you would make you ill. I had no idea he intended to kill you. Each time, he said he was sending you a warning. When I sensed the poison in your cup this last time, I knew his true intent, but by then it was too late. I had no control. My hands sent you a deadly brew."

Tears ran down Cassie's face. Conflicting emotions coursed through her blood. Compassion for the mistake Brianna made. Anger for the attempts on her life. Confusion as to why anyone would want to harm her. She swallowed. "I know it wasn't you. Not really, you, Brianna."

The spectre shook her head. "But, it was me. I allowed him to work through me. I gave him that power."

"Are you dead?" asked Jane as she walked around the apparition holding her right palm up, assessing the energy emanating from the being.

"I wish I was dead. But I am not. I never will be. After I fled through the back door of the kitchen, a cloaked figure grabbed my hand and squeezed it until all that was left of me was this, this echo of a life. He cast my essence to the wind. I am here and there and everywhere. I was only able to congeal into this image, because you were all thinking of me."

"We will think of you, again, Brianna," said Sanjay. "We will not forget you. You are one of us, now and forever and you will not be forgotten." He chanted quietly in Sanskrit

A smile broke on her lips. "When you hear the birds singing in the morning, think of me. It was my favorite part of the day."

"I wish we could reverse this," said Sanjay. "But we don't have that power."

"My soul will never be free. I am destined to feel regret, remorse, and failure for eternity. Let me be a lesson to all witches who dare to deal with demons. At least then, I can do some good."

"I forgive you," said Cassie, hoping with all her heart that the power of forgiveness could make a difference. "And I love you," she added.

Color infused the ghost's cheeks. "I am undeserving of both, but I am grateful."

Cassie lifted her chin. "I am grateful to have known you, Brianna. As are all the people in Mystic Keep. You made a difference. Your love touched many. I promise you, we will not forget you."

The long hair of the spectre turned red.

"We will hold a witch's celebration for you," said Sanjay.

The ghost's eyes blazed blue. She reached out as if to touch them, and vanished.

In the distance, sunlight broke through the clouds. The storm was over.

THIRTY-TWO

"Sometimes it takes a double shot of magic." ~ Sid

On the first stroke of midnight Cassie awoke to a buzzing sound. Fireflies filled her bedroom with their warm glow. The air felt warm and smelled of wildflowers. Classical guitar played somewhere in the distance. A wood fire crackled in her fireplace. "Sid, am I dreaming."

Sid purred and rolled over. "I'm out of here," she said and vanished.

A silver mist formed at the foot of her bed and Sanjay appeared. She wanted to rant at him about learning how to use a door, about letting her know when he was going to appear, about not assuming she wanted to see him, but she didn't. She couldn't ignore the wonderous, tingling sensation she had in the pit of her stomach. She wanted him.

Sanjay had done this for her, created a perfect space. She swallowed. How many women had he done this for, before her? Did she want to be another of his conquests? Could a rogue like Sanjay commit himself to a witch? Perhaps it would be wiser not to want him so so much.

"What now, warlock?" she said.

"Cassie." The fireflies flew out the window, leaving them in darkness save for the light of the full moon filtering through the window.

As he looked at her with a lover's eyes, her knees wobbled. "Please, tell me it's not about another checklist," she said.

He shook his head.

"Another app?"

He chuckled. Good goddess, even his laughter was sexy.

SANJAY HAD SPENT hours talking with Peregrine about how to create the most romantic entrance he could, until the falcon snored. That's what you get for talking to a bird, he had lamented. He chose to use things Cassie loved: a wood fire, the smell of wild flowers and moonlight. He added fire flies for himself. With magic he had created his entrance, the most important of his life.

Now he was totally lost.

Cassie stood before him in an oversized sweatshirt with The Perfect Brew logo on the front, and black lace panties beneath. Her long, shapely legs glowed in the moonlight. He swallowed. Cassie's unique mixture of the girl next door and vixen spelled him. Her green eyes flickered with magic like a siren's call to a sailor.

Ignoring her words, he took a step towards her.

CASSIE SUDDENLY FELT NAKED. The way his eyes heated up and took her in, made her quiver with need. There was no question why he was there. No question of his intent. The time for games was over. He wanted her, and she wanted him, even if he was a warlock.

She tossed her hair out of her face and blinked. "You're not saying anything."

"What do you want me to say?"

Anything. Something. Normally she felt sexually powerful with men, but not with Sanjay. He messed with her circuitry. "I thought we decided to keep things professional between us."

He stepped closer. She could smell his scent, the wild abandon of a warlock mixed with sea air and wilderness. Desire spiraled through her senses. She wanted to whimper. Maybe, they didn't need to talk. "Sanjay ..."

"You are the most frustrating woman I have ever met."

What! She glared at him.

Gently he brushed her hair out of her face. His touch ignited senses within her she didn't know she had. Leaning in, he said, "You are kind, caring and intelligent."

She pulled back, "If I ever need a job reference, I will be sure to call on you."

He laughed. "Yes, you are a fine choice for a mate. One that would please my grandmother and even the Brotherhood."

Cassie's cheeks burned. "I suppose that's a compliment."

Taking her hand in his he pulled her closer. "I also like how saucy you are."

"Saucy? Is there an app for that?"

"And sexy. Oh, so sexy."

"Mmm. Sanjay?"

He inhaled. "Okay, I'll just say it."

"That would be nice."

"I like your panties. A lot. The lace leaves me ... wondering." He grasped her hand and put it on his chest.

His heart beat strong, loud and fast. How could she question his sincerity? This was a warlock she could trust. "Sanjay ...."

He put a finger on her mouth and traced her full lips slowly. "You are the most intriguing woman I have ever met. He leaned in resting his forehead on hers. "The sexiest witch I have ever encountered." His hand reached for the small of her back. "And the most alluring sorceress in the world."

Red hot desire pulsed through her body. Cresting the wave of passion rode the love she felt for him and been denying. It flooded her very being. "Sanjay."

"My love, you have captured my heart. It is yours. I am yours."

She reached up and gently kissed him. "And I am yours."

Rose petals fell from the ceiling.

Sanjay kissed Cassie back. Thoroughly. They made it to the bed entwined in each other's arms, in one wicked warlock millisecond.

And they made sweet, sweet love. And then some.

Outside Sid joined Peregrine, who perched in a nearby tree under the light of the full moon. The weather in Mystic Keep had finally settled. They stood on guard for the rest of the night.

THIRTY-THREE

Coffee. "Black as the devil, hot as hell, pure as an angel, sweet as love."
~ Charles Maurice de Talleyrand

Vixen led the way up the trail to the Lookout, while Jane wandered slowly behind, soaking in the chatter of the trees. A salty breeze caressed her face, and the sun shone brilliantly in the endless sky. In the distance an eagle called his mate.

Jane marvelled at the calm after the storm. Living in a Pacific Rainforest wasn't like living anywhere else. The monumental changes in weather brought her closer to nature than she would have thought impossible. It gave her a sense of being a part of something much larger than the self.

When they got to the clearing, Jane snapped her fingers and their afternoon tea appeared on a table, complete with freshly baked scones, local blackberry jam and a variety of squares whose main ingredient was chocolate. Even business executives need to eat, thought Jane.

Vixen jumped up on the table and meowed her pleasure.

A pleasant tingling sensation crawled up her spine. Good fortune, she thought. Good fortune was coming her way.

As if on cue, the sound of hiking boots walking on the path caught her attention, and a moment later Brody appeared.

Ruggedly handsome as ever, he looked like he had jumped out of a Hallmark Christmas movie. His square jaw was nicely shadowed with scruff. Just like his cousin, his denim blue eyes glinting with mischief, and he had a lopsided smile that charmed her heart. As he neared, his woodsy scent flooded warmed her blood.

"Hubba-bubba, witch. He's taken," mumbled Vixen in her head.

"He's not married, yet," she responded.

"Don't say I didn't warn you," said the cat, before she jumped down to the ground, and climbed the nearest tree to watch the action.

Brody stood before Jane, six-feet of well-sculpted male perfection. She wanted to drool, but instead she tossed her hair behind her shoulders and gave him a direct look. "I didn't expect to see you here," she said.

He sat on the bench opposite her. "I thought I might find you here."

"Uh-huh."

"I could do with a cup of tea," he said.

She poured, and though the urge to lace it with magic was strong in her, she didn't. As she passed the cup over to him, she said, "Please, help yourself to the snacks."

"Snacks? This looks more like a feast." He took a scone,

and topped it with blackberry jam and whipped cream. "If we keep meeting like this, I'm going to end up fat."

If we keep meeting like this, I'm going to jump you, she thought. But she nodded. "I like it up here. It's a good place to think."

"How are your business plans going?"

"Mr. Shnit, the loans officer at the bank, says I need to draw up a better business plan. I've found a ton of step-by-step templates on line, but they're all so tedious. I decided I needed high tea."

He laughed. "If you want to run a business, you have to develop a certain mind set. Some of the work is boring but it has to be done."

Great, Mr. Handsome is lecturing me on work. We could use this time in the forest in so many more interesting ways. Jane licked whip cream off her top lip.

BRODY STARED AT HER. If only ... If only he wasn't engaged. "Maybe this isn't a good idea," he said. "I gotta go."

"No, please, stay."

"You know I'm getting married."

"And yet you keep turning up."

A Kingfisher chattered in a tree near the clearing. The surf crashed on the shore. The low bushes rustled with a squirrel searching for food. But Jane and Brody said nothing.

"I wish I could stay," he said. "I wish I could stay and get to know you better. With all my heart, I wish. But I can't."

"Why not?"

"It's complicated."

THIRTY-FOUR

"Hot, steamy, earth shattering, mind-blowing ... Coffee." ~
Koffee Addict, FB

Within days the lives of the mundane community of Mystic
Keep returned to normal. The dark cloud created by the
drug dealers lifted, and in its place a sense of calm spilled
through the streets. Ava told Cassie it was because the
Martians returned home. According to her, they had eaten
enough earthlings and wanted more diversity in their diet.
The Brew continued to draw new customers.

Kit organized a party for Larry at the community hall,
and all his friends turned up. Many shared stories about his
love for reading and bird watching, but mostly they talked
about his kindness. Larry had a way of making people feel
good about themselves, and that, thought Cassie, was a true
gift.

A donation pot was put on a side table, and by the end
of the event several hundred dollars had been collected.
Sanjay doubled the amount, and Kit donated it to the thrift
store in the church. Larry's last name remained a secret, as

did his real-life story, but in the end, they didn't matter. Everyone knew Larry for the man he was, a good man with a caring heart.

The church remained open 24/7 without a priest. It had more visitors than it had had in the last decade. People came and went, worshipping the divine in their own time.

On the supernatural front, lives calmed down as well. Gabriel O'Reilly became Sanjay's apprentice, shocking many in town. Sanjay had never imagined himself as a mentor, but now that his days as a rogue warlock were over, it seemed like a sensible thing to do. His ties to the Brotherhood became stronger every day, and a big ceremony of initiation was being planned by the powers that be.

The leaders of the search party: Hank Henderson, Pussy Nip, and Zatara of Xanadu formalized their groups into a supernatural police force, under Donovan O'Reilly's command. They called themselves the Mystic Warriors and they met regularly at The Keep to discuss the security of their growing town.

Cassie and Sanjay let everyone know about their last encounter with Brianna, about how they forgave her and how she hoped to be an example for others. The staff of The Perfect Brew held a celebration in her honor. Many tears were shed.

Stormy the sea-witch, continued to lay flowers below the headstone that marked Ophelia's earthly grave. Her ritual was as silent and mysterious as the woman below it. Cassie didn't ask questions. She figured in time, Stormy would tell her more about her great-aunt and their adventures.

And Sid, well, Sid was Sid. She spent her days lying in the windowsill basking in the rays of the sun, dreaming about tuna, anchovies and shiny things. Cassie thought she might be put-out by Sanjay being around so much, but it didn't seem to bother the cat at all.

Peregrine was another matter. Sid wasn't fond of the bird and the feelings were mutual, so there was an unspoken agreement that the familiars remained on their own home turfs as the lovers visited each other. Peregrine complained a lot, but he was a falcon.

As Sanjay and Cassie's combined-magic strengthened the wards around The Perfect Brew, the community of magical folk grew. Late at night when the coffee shop closed you could hear the sentient building sigh like a Momma Bear after a good day with her children. Ophelia's haven for supernatural beings had become a great success.

As long as no one thought about Erebus.

A COUPLE WEEKS after the showdown at the church, Cassie, Sanjay and Jane sat around the kitchen table in Cassie's apartment. Sid and Vixen lay together in the window sill snoozing. A steaming pot of freshly brewed coffee, and a platter of sliced meats and cheeses sat on the Lazy Susan between them. Jazz played over the speakers. Warm afternoon sunlight streamed through the windows. Their lives felt perfect, thought Cassie. Everything that needed to be said, had been said, and a feeling of calm companionship and deep love settled between them.

But fear clipped her thoughts. In her heart she knew all was not well, and would never be well, until they dealt with the Lord of Darkness. They couldn't go on, not talking about him.

Cassie spoke. "What good would I be dead?"

"Now that's a pleasant thought for a sunny day," muttered Jane as she heaped sugar in her brew.

"Seriously," Cassie said. "Erebus wants me dead. We all know that. But, why me?"

Sanjay's tiger eyes blazed. "The Lord of Darkness wants you dead because you're a powerful sorceress, my love. It's all about power. Dark versus light. You know the story. It's as old as time."

"Let's get real. I can barely boil water," said Cassie.

Sid chuckled.

Jane sneered. "Hey, you can't say that anymore. The old Cassie couldn't boil water, but don't play dumb with me. I saw what you did. You are one hex of a witch. I'd say great-aunt Ophelia left you more than a collection of coffee spoons. She opened a door for you into a new realm of magic, and you're rocking it."

"And these are only the early days," said Sanjay.

Cassie laughed. "I wish I could see what comes next. You know, peak around the corner."

"Speaking of that ...." Jane had waited for an opportunity to share her news, and this seemed as good a time as ever. "Mr. Shnits at the bank is looking over my business plan. With luck I could have the money to buy a van and my supplies by next week.

Sanjay narrowed his eyes. "Business plan? Why haven't I heard of this?"

"You can't be serious," said Cassie. "Mom and Dad won't approve."

Sanjay lifted his arms.

Jane said, "It's time for me to fly my own broom."

"And I'm not happy either," said Cassie. "I'd love you to live here, but this business idea is out of the question. How could you even think of doing it? You'll expose us all."

"Will someone fill me in?" said Sanjay.

"No, I won't." Jane tossed her curls. "Get over yourself

and have a little faith in me. I'm going to rock this town with my business. You know I'm good with people."

Sanjay's right brow rose. "What kind of business is this?"

"A witch business, of course," said Jane.

His left brow rose. "Witch business? Just what are you planning on doing, little one?"

"Helping people silly. I'm going to call it 1-300-I-Got-Witch."

Sanjay's face fell.

"Cute, eh," said Jane.

Sanjay ran a hand through his hair. "That's the craziest idea I've ever heard."

"Exactly," said Cassie. "You can't do it."

A DISTINCTIVE KNOCK came from the apartment's front door. Sanjay looked at Cassie who shrugged. The police had arrived.

"I'll get it," said Jane jumping up. "Gavin's too cute to leave waiting at the door."

Sanjay groaned, and wondered if he would ever get used to having a little sister.

As soon as Jane opened the door, Gavin strode into the room looking as ruggedly handsome as the first day Cassie had laid eyes on him. He wore blue jeans, and a soft plaid flannel shirt that brought out the cobalt blue in his eyes.

"Do I have to be here?" asked Sanjay.

"Please, stay," said Gavin. "I have something to tell all of you."

"Coffee?" asked Cassie.

"No, thanks. I don't trust ..." He stopped and chuckled. "I know you guys do something to the coffee around here. I always suspected it, and now I know it. I want to stay ..." A deep v formed between his eyes as he searched for the word.

"Sane? Normal? Sober? What is it you want to stay, detective?" asked Jane.

Gavin put his hands on his hips, the way football coaches standing on the sidelines do, and cleared his throat. "I came to thank you all for your help with my investigation. Thanks to you, the drug ring is busted, the murderer is in jail and the citizens of Mystic Keep are safe."

"You're welcome," said Cassie waving her hand to dismiss his formal speech. "What's bothering you?" Clearly, something was.

"I don't like that I've been given credit for the whole affair. You guys saved the day, but considering your use of magic, which we all agree needs to stay hidden, I accepted the credit. I don't think it would help any of us, if the news of your abilities got out."

Sanjay stood and reached out to shake Gavin's hand. "Detective, it was an honor to work with you. You deserve accommodations for your effort. Truly, you are an exceptional policeman, and we couldn't have done it without you."

Gavin looked at the warlock's hand and hesitated. It was, of course, the same hand that streaks of lightening had shot out of a few days before. He gritted his teeth and shook Sanjay's hand.

Cassie winked at him. "Yes, I agree. You are exceptional. Thank you for coming to my rescue. I'll never forget your bravery."

Gavin's face reddened. "I'm up for an accommodation, which is kind of a big deal, but I have to tell ya, it doesn't feel right. I didn't solve the murder, or run the drug dealers to the ground."

"Maybe not, exactly," said Jane. "But you played an important role, and you kept the supernatural aspect of the whole affair safely out of the view of regular folk. That's important. You've kept the peace. Isn't that your main job?"

Gavin looked down at Jane's wide blue eyes. His aw-shucks grin turned up on one side, and his coloring returned to normal. "I could get used to having you around."

They all laughed.

"There's one thing that still bothers me," said Gavin.

"What's that?" asked Sanjay.

"Who wrote the note in Larry's hand, and what did it mean? A man shot in the heart two times doesn't write a note."

"BEWARE BLACK WITCH," said Cassie. "I've thought a lot about it. I figure it had to be Erebus, sticking his black magic in where he could."

Jane nodded. "That makes sense."

Sanjay said nothing for a few seconds. "I don't know. It still bothers me. It's as if someone planted the note to draw attention to Cassie. I don't think it was related to Larry's death at all. It could have been Erebus, or it could have been someone else who found an opportunity to attack her. We need to be careful."

"Enough already, you guys," said Jane. "Lighten up. We won. Let's enjoy our victory."

Cassie shrugged. "I agree with you for once, Jane. I'm getting used to living with uncertainty. It's the way our world spins. I'm all for savouring the good times when they come my way." She smiled at Sanjay.

Gavin took a step towards Jane. "Talking about good times. I hear my cousin, Brody, is quite bewitched by you. If you harm one hair on his head, you'll have to answer to me."

Jane saluted him. "Yes, sir. I hear you. I didn't use

magic, and for the record I felt bewitched, as well. It's just too bad he's taken."

The cop nodded slowly, and looked as if he had something more to say about the matter, but before he could, a knock resounded on the door.

JANE ANSWERED it to find a flower box left on the floor outside. With a flick of her wrist she opened it to see a bouquet and a note. "This is interesting," she said as she walked them in, "Black flowers."

Sid snickered.

Sanjay gave a guttural warlock groan. Not a pleasant sound, thought Cassie.

Jane placed the box on the counter and returned to her seat.

Cassie didn't need to look at the card to know who they came from. The only person she knew who sent black flowers was Alessandro, and then only on special occasions. The flowers sent a chill up her spine. How many times had she told him they were over? She didn't have enough fingers to count.

Gavin took one look around at the faces and said, "There's never a dull moment around here. I'll be on my way." As he slid through the open door, he added, "An inspector from Interpol has been trying to reach me and I need to return her call."

Cassie swallowed hard and with a flick of her wrist, banished the flowers out of sight.

"I thought you talked to Alessandro," Sanjay said to Cassie.

"I did. He's not a good listener." She sighed. "I'll tell him again."

Their eyes locked. "Do that," said Sanjay rising from his seat.

"You don't have to go," said Cassie.

"I need to get my place ready for the party tonight," Sanjay said. He had invited all the supernaturals who formed the search parties looking for Brianna to thank them for their efforts.

"I ordered beer, wine, and champagne," he explained. "Five kitchen witches are cooking up a feast in my kitchen. There will be lobster, steak, duck, and you name it. Every search member's fantasy meal will be served. I've left Peregrine to watch over everything, but I should be there."

Jane put her mug down. "What does George, that ghost of yours, think of all of this?"

Sanjay grinned. "I thought it might upset him, but I was wrong. He's excited about having a party at his house. I don't think he understands that he's not the main attraction."

"I can't wait for it to start. I love warlock parties," said Jane. "But first I have some things to do."

Sanjay narrowed his eyes at Jane. "What are you up to, little one?"

"Magic!" She wiggled her nose and vanished, leaving Cassie and Sanjay alone.

"MAGIC," Cassie said looking deeply into Sanjay's orange eyes.

"Magic," said Sanjay raising a brow.

Sid purred.

AFTERWORD

Dear Readers,

I hope you enjoyed Cassie's adventures as much as I did. Her story continues in the third and final book in the trilogy, A Triple Shot of Trouble.

I would love it, if you would take a few moments and spread the word about my books. You can review them on any of the sales platforms you buy them from. As they say, sharing means caring. Your reviews mean the world to me, and help other readers find my books.

If you want to know more about me, check out my website: https://www.Jo-AnnCarson.com. There you can find all my social media links.

If you want to follow my latest news, read carefully selected excerpts, find book deals and enter contests, join my newsletter, (https://jo-anncarson.com/free-book-offer/). You will receive a free novella when you sign up.

Warmest Regards,

Jo-Ann

ACKNOWLEDGMENTS

I'd like to thank:

My beta readers who keep me on track:

Barb Cassata
Nicole Laverdure
Marianne Kay
Darcy Speed

My proofreader who polishes my work:

Tammy Payne

And my cover designers:

Deranged Doctor Design

THE PERFECT BREW TRILOGY

All buy links can be found on my website: https://www.Jo-AnnCarson.com

The Perfect Brew
A potion for mystery & magic

When evil rises one clumsy witch must save the world. Cassie Black inherits a sentient coffee-house, complete with an inter-dimensional portal and a side of ancient curse from her great-aunt Ophelia. When Cassie attends the funeral, she discovers the Pacific Northwest town is a haven for supernatural beings. Ophelia's death is suspicious and her lawyer is poisoned.

Up to her neck in mysteries, and weighed down with a mysterious curse, Cassie hunts for the murderer. There are many unusual suspects, a tall, dark and annoying detective keeps getting in her way, and a seductive warlock offers his assistance.

Will Cassie catch the villain before he kills again? Can she protect the portal and still free herself from the curse?

Will Sid, her snarky cat familiar, convince her to play dirty with the boys?

This is the first novella in The Perfect Brew, paranormal, cozy series, which can be read as a stand-alone. If you like stories with strong characters, cozy-styled mystery and humor, you'll love this one. There's no sex or violence on the page, but be prepared for some serious romance, mystery, and magic.

Buy *The Perfect Brew* today to start your own magical adventure in the town of Mystic Keep.

A Triple Shot of Trouble

~ Trouble comes in threes

Can an enchantress stop evil from taking over the world? In the third book in the Perfect Brew trilogy, Cassie Black, a powerful witch with a serious caffeine addiction, faces Erebus, The Lord of Darkness who has no weaknesses because he's a pure badass. With the help of a sexy warlock, a vampire who doesn't understand the word "no," and a very-human detective, she searches for a way to banish the Master of Evil forever.

It's been months since the dark lord raised his head, but when an artist in town is murdered, Cassie knows the beast is back. Using all her resources, she searches for her friend's murderer knowing they will lead to the source of all evil.

Will the body count rise before Cassie catches the killer? Will she vanquish Erebus once and for all? It's a good thing her coffee's spiked with magic, because she has a lot on her plate.

A Triple Shot of Trouble is the third and final book in the critically acclaimed Perfect Brew trilogy. It can be read as a stand-alone or as part of the series. If you like magical cozies with strong characters, romance, and humor, you'll love this novel. It has a happy ending.

Buy *A Triple Shot of Trouble,* today and enjoy a fun, heart-warming story filled with intrigue, sweet romance and a touch of magic.

Death by Tarot Card

The Gambling Ghosts Series (2016, 2017)

(sweet fantasy, adventure and romance)

A Highland Ghost for Christmas, Novella #1

A Valentine's Ghost for Valentine's Day, Novella # 2

Confessions of a Pirate Ghost, Novella #3

The Biker Ghost Meets His Match, Novella #4

The Vancouver Blues Series

(Steamy Romantic Suspense)

Black Cat Blues

Ain't Misbehavin'

Mata Hari Series

(Steamy Romantic Suspense)

Covert Danger

Ancient Danger

Lovin' Danger

ABOUT THE AUTHOR

Jo-Ann Carson
Storytelling is her lifestyle.

Reports of Jo-Ann Carson's death on a far-away island are greatly exaggerated or, at the very least, premature. She's an award-winning fiction author, blogger and podcaster.

In Jo-Ann Carson's stories everything goes bump in the night or takes a bite. In her latest trilogy, **The Perfect Brew**, Cassie Black inherits an enchanted coffee house from her eccentric great-aunt where every cup is served with a side of magic. Unfortunately, she also inherits a curse and dead bodies pile up around her. A wickedly sexy warlock, a possessive vampire and a straight-shooting human cop vie for her attention. To date, Jo-Ann has published 20 titles. Current buy links can be found on her website.

A firm believer in the magic of our everyday lives, Jo-Ann loves watching sunrises, walking beaches near her home in the Pacific Northwest and reading by the fire.

Website: https://www.Jo-AnnCarson.com

Bookbub: https://www.bookbub.com/profile/jo-ann-carson

Goodreads: https://www.goodreads.com/author/show/13499849.Jo_Ann_Carson

Facebook: https://www.facebook.com/JoAnnCarsonAuthor

Twitter: https://twitter.com/Jo_AnnCarson

Pinterest: https://www.pinterest.ca/authorjoanncarson/

www.ingramcontent.com/pod-product-compliance
Lightning Source LLC
Chambersburg PA
CBHW030136180626
46812CB00002B/713